T0244713

hello, world? © Anna Poletti, 2024

Published by Semiotext(e)
PO BOX 629, South Pasadena, CA 91031
www.semiotexte.com

Cover Photograph by Samantha Arnull
Cover Design: Lauren Mackler
Layout: Aldon Chen

ISBN: 978-1-63590-229-7

Distributed by the MIT Press, Cambridge, Mass.,
and London, England
Printed and bound in the United States of America.

10 9 8 7 6 5 4 3 2 1

hello, world?

Anna Poletti

Semiotext(e)

Table of Contents

So if we are visited in our state by someone who has the skill to transform themself into all sorts of characters and represent all sorts of things, and they want to show off themself and their poems to us, we shall treat them with all the reverence due to a priest and giver of rare pleasure, but shall tell them that they and their kind have no place in our city, their presence being forbidden by our code, and send them elsewhere, after anointing them with myrrh and crowning them.

—Plato, "Education: The First Stage," *The Republic*

Prologue: Honesty

They are walking together in the low light of early spring. The kind of light that tells Dutch people it's safe to smile after months of grimacing into the bitter northerly wind that propels horizontal rain. H and Seasonal are taking one of their usual Sunday midmorning walks. It is the kind of walk that might end with a piece of cake, or with fresh sourdough bread from the farmer's market. They've been living in their new apartment for four months. The mortgage payments are still a monthly shock. Seasonal's job at the university can cover the payments comfortably enough, but the two of them have only been living in Europe for eighteen months and everything still feels either new in an exciting way or new in a completely disorienting way. Together, Seasonal and H are cobbling together the next phase of their lives. Seasonal has been in a bit of a daze since they arrived here. She has achieved what she had thought was impossible. When she met H twelve years ago as a twenty-nine-year-old woman with a freshly minted PhD whose mother did not finish high school, Seasonal had been aimlessly moving around the East Coast of Australia wondering what was going to happen to her next. What had happened was a lot better than she thought a girl like her was allowed to expect. A beautiful man with blue eyes, who liked to laugh and had a sharp intelligence. Who treated her as an equal, and taught her how to look at (and more importantly, dismiss) art. A man who recognized Seasonal's struggle to imagine a life beyond the very narrow parameters she was given as a working-class kid from a small town full of white people. Seasonal's first book was published. She presented at conferences and made collegial intellectual friendships. Articles were accepted … holy shit, was Seasonal building a career? No one had ever talked to her about how to do that, she was making it up as she went along. And now, twelve years later, here she was, an associate professor. The career had done the thing Seasonal had wanted but had not dared to admit to anyone until H and his blue eyes had arrived; it had given her the means to leave Australia. But really, it was H's love that had made Seasonal think she could face the struggle of being a foreigner. Being an alien while walking around inside his love is a gift.

H and Seasonal are walking in step. Their jackets zipped against the cold, scarfs wrapped high. As usual, they are talking about their writing. They talk about the things they are reading or, in H's case, have stopped reading halfway through because he has abandoned completism. They pat the cats who are seeking the spring sun on the narrow footpaths outside the small Dutch houses. A comfortable silence emerges. As it lengthens, Seasonal realizes: *This is my moment.*

Seasonal has been practicing the question in her mind for months. Revising and editing it with more diligence than she brings to the sentences in her academic writing. Seasonal knows the question, and its delivery, needs to sound soft and open, even though the sentence terrifies her. She is hoping the question is an invitation, not a detonation.

There is something I wanted to ask you about, Seasonal says, trying to sound calm, as they approach the canal that rings the old city of Utrecht.

Shoot, H responds breezily.

There is a lull in the walk. A small group of cyclists cruises past. The crocuses are starting to peep.

I am hoping we can talk about sex, she says, glancing at him. Seasonal wonders if he might speak, admit relief or joy. Instead, he keeps his eyes on the traffic. He is silent.

Do you think we might be able to start having sex again? There. She's said it. Fear puts a small vibration in her voice. Can he hear it?

Oh … H turns his face away from Seasonal to check the gap in the traffic so they can cross the street.

No. I am not interested in sex anymore, he says, calmly, as their feet meet the wet path along the canal.

Oh … Seasonal tries to match his tone. Panic courses through her body.

And what do you think that means for me? Was it panic, or rage? She can't tell.

I hadn't thought about that, comes the honest, cool response.

His answer clarifies her feeling. Rage. How could he have not thought about her? Seasonal wants to pull the next passing cyclist from their bicycle and punch them.

They keep walking in silence. H is thinking. Seasonal is disintegrating.

I guess this means we should open our relationship. So you can have sex with other people.

He sounds so reasonable. So calm. A month later, Seasonal realizes it was not calm she was hearing, but death. H's sexuality had died. His desire, gone. But at this moment, when she hears it for the first time, she mistakes death for openness and willingness to collaborate. This is how he had always been with her. Until now. Now his position is fixed. He identifies as asexual.

It's like a steam burn. Brief, sharp, bright pain. Over and over. It runs across Seasonal's entire body. Each time in the coming months when she tries to probe the site of H's now-dead desire, another layer of her being is wounded. She becomes a giant blister. Puffed up and empty and fragile and awkward. Each time she asks, H looks her in the eye, the way he does when he is facing the truth, and tries to explain why he identifies as asexual. For a decade, walks like the one that fateful Sunday would end in hours in bed followed by a late lunch. *Why do people even have sex?* he asks now, and the question is genuine, or at least, the asking is. Seasonal burst into tears. She does not know how to answer, but she sees the truth on his face. Seasonal's vulnerability, her hunger and need, does not interest H anymore. He still wants her to read drafts of his next book. He still wants to sing small songs about nothing while he tidies up after breakfast, and he will still laugh with her. But he does not want to be the portal through which Seasonal can cautiously approach the horror and joy of existence in all its enormity and randomness. He has become the randomness.

It's like a steam burn. He is denouncing them. Here, on the continent where she knows no one but him and his angry mother whom he was trying to forgive for being scarred by her childhood in the Hunger Winter. Here, in the country where he had been born but had not lived for over thirty years. They had come here together. But now H seemed to have no choice but to leave Seasonal to her fate.

And so Seasonal had to accept that H no longer wanted to want. She was suddenly alone in her need. She had to go out into the world with her desire, and without the gift of his love. She was going to have to be brave in ways she could not anticipate.

Algorithms and Surprises

From Wikipedia:

A "Hello, World!" program is a computer program that outputs or displays "Hello, World!" to a user. Being a very simple program in most programming languages, it is often used to illustrate the basic syntax of a programming language for a working program, and as such is often the very first program people write.

(They learn this from the Russian.)

Seasonal has lived in the Netherlands for two years. Their world is very small. But as things break apart, they manage to assemble a small chorus of witnesses to whom they describe their experiences.

M: A writer living in Massachusetts. They were sort of friends with Seasonal before each left Australia; the friendship has been strengthened by the shared experience of being away from home. They communicate almost exclusively through voice messages, which are kind of letters, in WhatsApp.

Y: Seasonal's friend of twenty years. Artist, mother, teacher, living on a slither of land beside the Pacific Ocean.

Q: A transmasc poet, scholar, writer. He writes and thinks with Seasonal from his home in Melbourne, Australia.

C: Their only Dutch friend. Smart, weird, a pianist. Recovering from the abrupt end of her marriage to the father of her teenage son.

J: A German associate professor of gender studies with a brain Seasonal loves.

One gloomy winter morning, when they should have been sleeping, Seasonal downloads the dating app and starts a profile. After some precursory research into dating and hookup apps, they choose one that is renowned for its algorithm, which is underpinned by an enormous number of questions. Many of the questions were developed by users in the early days of the service, and have subsequently been augmented with what Seasonal suspects are carefully calibrated questions designed by in-house psychologists. Seasonal spends many hours allowing the app to interrogate them. Sitting on the toilet, in the bath, stirring food on the cooktop, on trains to and from Amsterdam, when they should be doing their Dutch homework, Seasonal invents opinions and expresses ones they really possess on all manner of issues. They often laugh out loud at the phrasing and the specificity of the questions: Could you be in a relationship with a messy person? Could you date someone who owns a gun? A snake? Thirty guitars or 250 pairs of sneakers? Could you date someone with different political views than you? Who is religious if you are not?

Answering these questions makes Seasonal fall in love with humanity again.

The picture they set as the landing image of their profile is a selfie they took two years ago. They are smiling into the tiny camera, wearing a bright-red duffle coat and a grey scarf. Their short, undyed hair shows enough grey to make anyone think twice before complimenting Seasonal for looking *young for their age*. Their deep brown eyes glow with the mix of joy and conspiracy that they like to imagine is their signature mood. Over their shoulder, the viewer of the selfie can see two women with similarly short hair. One wears a well-fitting and well-worn leather jacket, the other a turquoise outdoor jacket commonly sold in hiking stores. The woman in the turquoise jacket stands in front of the other, at a short distance, framing a tightly cropped portrait in front of a wall made of grey cinder blocks. These two women are Seasonal's friends who are also colleagues, but the viewer of Seasonal's selfie wouldn't know it. Seasonal is smiling so easily and happily because they are showing their friends one of their favorite places in their home city of Melbourne. It is a sunny Melbourne winter day in the photograph, and looking at it in the dark Dutch winter, Seasonal likes the happiness they see on their own face, and the clearness in their eyes. They envy that person who was them.

In the open text box in the app where Seasonal can write a self-description, they enter: *feminist. writer. likes to walk.*

Seasonal also spends five minutes setting up a profile on a hookup app which has no interest in interrogating them. This one is all about the photographs. With these two rods in the water, they wait.

In the coming weeks and months, Seasonal makes all kinds of connections using the apps. The profiles they chat with include:

The slut: Freelance merger expert. Usually a dom, he discovers a strong need to be humiliated by Seasonal. Forty-seven years old, Belgian, he is cheating on his jealous submissive girlfriend because *she does not understand my submissive side.*

The Sound Engineer: Bisexual aikido blackbelt and portrait photographer. In the final stages of starting his new life, ethical nonmonogamist. Father of five children.

The Parisian: Workaholic design director and visual artist. Very witty, submissive, strong aesthetic, reads a lot of fiction. *I can't stay ugly things*, he tells Seasonal when he sends them a picture of the matte-black dildo he hopes they will fuck him with.

The Russian: Expat with Dutch citizenship. A forty-one-year-old IT professional. Started dating after his wife spent a year telling him the marriage was over. Still living in the family home. Estranged from Russia, although his wife regularly travels there.

D: Trans man, forty-seven years old. Does not like Seasonal as much as they want him to. Frustratingly illusive, with a generous laugh.

László: Hungarian based in Amsterdam. His dating profile says he is thirty-eight, which his professional profile reveals to be inaccurate by eight years. He also lists himself as single on his profile, but he is actually in a committed, cohabiting relationship with the mother of his ten-year-old son, whom he will later refer to as his *partner*. László openly advertises his bisexuality and interest in BDSM on his dating profile alongside a picture of Michel Foucault. Smart, proud, deeply invested in his autonomy but looking to submit.

F.: Queer American woman who moved to the Netherlands for a woman seven years ago. Experimenting with polyamory because her new partner is poly and she needs to even things out.

Odysseus: Tall and thin and beautifully dressed in the photographs on his Tinder profile, which reads: *INFJ, 1.93 cm sapiosexual giant. Creative, a bit crazy and unconventional.* Amongst the many pictures on his profile there is a black-and-white image of a man sitting beside a clawfoot bathtub reading to a woman with short hair as she bathes. In his profile he says, *The bathroom picture is not me, but a complicity that ignites my mind. You?*

The composer: Iranian who has lived in the Netherlands for twelve years. Forty-five years old, has been in love once, with his Spanish ex-wife who is now his best friend.

First Man: Pakistani raised in the north of England, now working in Amsterdam. Father of two girls. Thinks Seasonal's English is *impressively good.* Asks them to explain intersectional feminism, and shortly afterward asks them repeatedly if they *are ready for a man to fall in love with you?*

The Pianist: Is vaguely recognizable from his profile pictures, which cover a wide range of hairstyles and ages. He makes his living teaching musicians how to improvise. He says he was married to a *narcissist,* but Seasonal wonders if he was married to a feminist. When Seasonal asks him about teaching improvisation to musicians, he manages to explain improvisation as the learning of structure. Of course this question is really about sex and he seems not to have noticed. His answer, and his inability to decode the flirtation, sink his prospects entirely.

A few weeks after joining the apps, Seasonal is drafting the acknowledgements for their book and trying to work out how to thank the slut, whose sexually explicit text messages via the dating app have gotten them through the final month of writing.

Sitting at their desk, the cheapest IKEA dining table in white Formica, wedged into the unused kitchen on the second floor of their apartment, they wonder: *Is there an essay to be written about the erotic messages sent between two strangers in their forties on a dating app?* They are using the slut to get their book finished. It is the book they thought they had to write to get out of Australia. Now that they are out, they are finding it hard to finish. Meeting the slut in person has become the reward for getting the manuscript done. He has obediently agreed to wait, and so they send flirtatious and then filthy messages back and forth, testing and tallying their sexual compatibility. Seasonal masturbates every day in the shower, as it is the only place they have complete privacy from H. The sexual tension and near-constant state of arousal the slut has them in is giving them the energy to finish the book, and they are shamelessly using him. They are interested in how useful they are finding sexual desire for unblocking their intellectual-creative process. *But then again*, they think one day walking home from the university along the quiet outer streets of the city, *it seems really fucking obvious that not having sex for nearly two years would make writing hard.*

Not long into their chat with the slut, he tells Seasonal he wants to be owned by them. No one has ever proposed this to Seasonal before. The minute they read the message, they realize they want to own someone very badly.

The slut works himself into a fever every day sending messages proclaiming his preparedness to be humiliated, instructed, disciplined, cuckolded, and to worship them. They ask him to tell them exactly what *owning him* means. He writes a list.

The rules for my Mistress

If my Mistress decides to own me she will
get my body and mind …

This means that my cock, balls, and
everything belongs to you …
even if it is in another pussy …
even in my GF's pussy …

You can punish me or reward me
if you like, you decide as my
Mistress … I will serve my Mistress
at her discretion

I want to work to a complete D/s
relationship in which degradation / pain / lust
and obedience plays a role …
Make me your puppy
your slut boy …

Your pleasure comes first always ...

I know I still have to learn
a lot but I hope you can teach
me ...

Most important is that I want to
please you, Mistress!!

The slut's list terrifies him.

Everything he says makes perfect sense to Seasonal. But they have no idea why. A newfound will to power surges in their blood, in the muscles in their legs, in the hair on the back of their neck. Their body is singing and shouting in a voice it has never used before. Confusion and arousal mix in their lungs.

After a perfunctory first date of drinks (him: three nonalcoholic beers; them: fresh mint tea and two bottles of sparkling water), Seasonal's second date with the Sound Engineer is a trip to a large national park on land the Dutch reclaimed from the sea in the mid-1960s. He wants to go to the park to see if they can spot the baby foxes that have been sighted there. The park is called the Oostvaardersplassen. Later, when they try to tell C where they went, Seasonal cannot pronounce this word. The original plan for the land was that it would be an industrial park. The industry never arrived, nature took over, and the pragmatic Dutch made it into a national park. Or at least this is the origin story the Sound Engineer tells them, on the one-hour drive from the suburban train station where they met.

It is early in the Dutch spring and has been raining for days. The lack of people and buildings as far as the eye can see is refreshing and beautiful. Seasonal misses Australia for the first time. When the trees and earth are this wet in Australia, they release the sharp, sweet smell of eucalyptus. Here, the air here is damp but not fragrant. Their nose misses home. They walk deep into the park and stand with the Sound Engineer in a raised hexagonal birdwatching hide. The two of them appear to have the park to themselves because it is Friday evening and the weather is terrible: the rain comes down in sheets, and the sky is low. After standing in the hide for at least twenty minutes, they see a fox crossing the fields on the other side of a canal which borders the edge of the park. It moves fast, but appears to be only walking. Tail hanging low. Seasonal is used to seeing foxes—in Australia they're pests that kill everyone's chickens, eat the small native mammals, and were regularly spotted in the paddocks next to their childhood home. But here is a fox where it is supposed to be. It is wildlife, not a feral pest. They are on its turf now.

After the fox disappears quickly into the distance, more quickly than they think is plausible, another one appears just below them, right outside the hide. It holds a duck in its mouth. The Sound Engineer moves outside into the rain with the same stealth as the animal. Seasonal follows him.

Together they watch the fox walk low and fast to a clutch of fallen logs and bury the body. They return to the hide to get out of the rain, and kiss. The Sound Engineer runs his hands under Seasonal's black cashmere jumper. He lifts it and finds their small breasts. They briefly flirt, should they fuck here? The Sound Engineer makes a joke about Dutch birdwatchers with telescopic lenses. They walk back to the car in the pouring rain. They each smoke on the way. He is drenched to the bone: *So nervous about our meeting*, he tells them, *I forgot my raincoat.*

On the drive back to Utrecht they discuss the possibility of going to his photographic studio and fucking on the inflatable bed he has there. Seasonal can hear the slut (who has strong cuckolding fantasies) shrieking with glee. They almost agree just to be able to tell him about it. They have told the Sound Engineer some complicated lie about why they can't spend the night together. With his tongue in their mouth they completely forget why they needed it.

Along with the astonishing prospect of owning the slut, Seasonal discovers the new pleasures of deleting and ignoring.

A few weeks later, the weather is still soggy and Seasonal is back in the car with the Sound Engineer. They have no idea where they are. He has met them at a suburban train station, and now the GPS is guiding him along a motorway. Seasonal loads Google Maps and gazes at the little blue dot moving along the road. They see Utrecht, somewhere to the south, but feel no sense of location, no sense of place.

He has arranged an Airbnb for their first night together—a self-contained unit on a farm. It is secluded from the old farmhouse with its high thatched roof by an impressive hedge. The woman in her early sixties who greets them and shows them the accommodation appears jovial and asks no questions.

The Sound Engineer is offering Seasonal emplacement through the Oostvaardersplassen: they went there before the drive to the farmhouse, and they return there in the morning. It appears to be their start and end place. In the morning, when they arrive at the park and pull over on the side of the road, near a fence that keeps the wild horses off the road, Seasonal asks him about the bird they hear but cannot see. They are trying to learn the birds. The reed singer is a tiny brown thing, almost invisible, with an extraordinarily complicated song and confident voice. They sing the reeds but also make it seem as though the reeds themselves are singing.

As they walk into the waterlogged park, the Sound Engineer is constantly scanning the environment for birds. Seasonal lazily looks at the trees and the sky. They try to stop seeing Australia and see the Netherlands. This land reclaimed from the sea that was supposed to be a site of mid-twentieth-century industry: he remembers it being drawn on the map at school and he was amazed his country could expand this way, that new parts of it could be built out of the sea. They try not to see Australia and to see where they are. To see the trees, low and full, and the sky, which is low too. They are getting better at it.

Who you are is the average of the five people you spend the most time with, who are most important to you, he tells them as they walk toward a different hide, set on the edge of a marsh.

Seasonal says nothing. They are replaying in their mind's eye the aikido move he used to take their hand off his cock the night before. *Aikido works with energy rather than against it,* he told them as they smoked together on the small veranda of the cabin and enjoyed the prospect of being naked together. He had used their desire to touch him to stop them from touching him. *So efficient, so gentle,* they thought. Seasonal would like to learn to direct the world this way.

Seasonal agrees with the slut that their second date should be an audition. They book a room at a four-star hotel near their apartment and tell him to meet them there. His audition will involve him performing oral sex on them, to see if they like his technique. He claims he will make them *cum in ten minutes.*

The slut passes the audition, but they do not let him take off his jeans. His erection straining under the distressed denim. After an hour, and some genuine pleasure on their part, Seasonal dismisses him. He leaves the room and they take a shower.

A few days later, via the chat function in the app (which he prefers, despite the clunky interface and slow refresh rate, so that his girlfriend can't see his messages), the slut tells them about his fantasy: Seasonal phones him and instructs him to drive them somewhere, and when he comes to collect them, they sit in the back seat of his BMW and refuse to let him touch them. When the car arrives at the destination, they lift their skirt and show him their *wet pussy*. They get out of the car and walk away.

Apart from the skirt, this sounds like a great idea to Seasonal.

They arrange for him to collect them at a park near their apartment and drive them to Amsterdam for a first date with someone else Seasonal has met on the app. He is late.
I'm sorry I am late, Mistress, the traffic was very bad, he says as he steps out of this BMW.

He wants to kiss them. Seasonal instinctively pulls back from him, and gets into the front seat of the low, brown car. The conversation flows easily all the way to Amsterdam. He smells good, and when their eyes briefly meet while he drives there is strong chemistry. Soon enough he is navigating the car down the narrow streets of the Jordaan to the café where Seasonal will meet the chef for a date. They thank him for the ride and get out of the car.

Hope you have fun, Mistress, he texts as he drives away.

The date with the chef is better than it should be because the slut drove them there.

As spring progresses, Seasonal rides the high-speed train to London to attend a conference. The Sound Engineer says via WhatsApp that he wants to photograph them. They ask to see his work. He texts them images he says he has permission to share. The male gaze. The female form. Lingerie. Beds. Mesh curtains. His aesthetic is pedestrian and excruciatingly heterosexual for a man who likes to fuck men. Seasonal feels the sharp disappointment of realizing their aesthetics are not complementary.

But they are writing about him, and so isn't it fair that he takes pictures of them?

Later, the Parisian will describe exactly how they should be photographed and it will shock them.

And still later they will see another potential photograph, under the bad lighting of the Hotel Le Dome in Brussels, when their torso is covered in their menstrual blood.

But for now Seasonal offers a casual, noncommittal answer, the kind women who fear the violence of men perfect very early in their time on the earth.

In these strange, wet months, the tantalizing possibility of dominance emerges from the fog of confusion and sadness. Their neck muscles gleefully hold Seasonal's head high. Their gaze finds a new level of penetration. They see power in new places, in entirely new forms. They see men wandering around with their desires in their hands, on their screens, asking plaintively and not always clearly ... Seasonal cannot quite decode what they're saying. But their curiosity is becoming boundless.

Seasonal thinks that summer is almost here, but they have made that mistake before. The students are almost gone from the university, and their colleagues spend more time talking about their holiday plans than their stress. The sun has some heat in it finally, and Seasonal sits on the small balcony of their apartment, chatting with a Scotsman who is visiting Amsterdam. They exchange a few polite messages, then he asks, out of the blue:

Can I ask you—I'm getting
a kink vibe from you.
Would it be OK to ask
if that's true?

> *is it the short hair that is*
> *giving you that vibe? ;)*

A bit ... and I'm wondering
if you're toward the Top/D
end of things. Or at least
Switch. It's my Spider Senses.
Or Kink-Dar.

> *ha! spot on.*

Seasonal knows this is a bold statement for someone who has only managed to audition and dismiss an expert in corporate mergers. But they make it anyway.

En route to the Sound Engineer's apartment: their fourth date. A kind of booty call. The days are getting longer, and they watch the light changing as they cycle to the train station.

They can barely bring themself to get on the train when it pulls into the platform. Seasonal looks at the other travelers, wondering if anyone else is using this early-evening train as a transportation device into the unknown. To calm their nerves, to fortify themself against the fear that bounces in their chest cavity, they type frantically into the Notes app on their phone:

Trying not to fear
Trying to stay open
Trying to find the courage to work against the inner structures that tell me that I am going to die he is going to kill me I am going to have a terrible time it is going to be boring I am going to wish I was at home on the couch watching another episode of Queer Eye *with H. He has no respect for you he is going to fuck you like a whore and not in a way that you would like and you are going to crawl back home to your apartment begging H for forgiveness*

This is the voice of my mother
This is the voice of the patriarchy
This is the voice that keeps me inside and celibate for the next twenty years

This is what I have to overcome to live

On their second or third date, the Sound Engineer had said, when talking about aikido, *I know how to stand in my power.*

Aikido is a third way between submissiveness and attacking: no resistance, but a redirection of energy from the other person.

Waiting for the kettle to boil the next morning, Seasonal asks themself: *If we can stand in our power, how do we stand in our ambivalence?*

As the European summer begins to ripen, Y, who has not been in Europe for twenty-two years, arrives for a visit with her nine-year-old daughter. As they travel together to Berlin, Bilbao, Amsterdam, the trio pass as a picture-perfect rainbow family; next to Y's petite-femme style, Seasonal's androgyny looks butch.

Unbeknownst to the two artsy women in their forties, their trip to Paris coincides with France being in the final for the World Cup and it is Bastille Day.

It is hot. Y sets the itinerary. Their first evening in the hotel near Gare de Lyon, Seasonal opens the hookup app on their phone for entertainment while they smoke in the courtyard with Y. Soon enough, they are chatting with the Parisian.

The banter is good. He offers a character sketch:

Ying and yang
Boyish and girly
Proud and submitted
Happy and deep
I like contrast
:)

:)
nice list

hihi

Chatting with the slut has taught them to read the clues. They tell the Parisian he looks like *such a good boy* in his pics, and they have him. The next day they have his phone number and, as they watch people dancing salsa beside the Seine in the evening light, Seasonal orders him to get in the shower and make himself *nice and clean* for them.

Over the next few days they message almost constantly but don't meet: France's win in the World Cup chokes Paris in traffic and crowds. Instead of meeting in person they spend the evening trading pictures and describing a variety of sexual acts they might try together. He wants them to fuck him with the double dildo he has bought, but he is afraid of its size.

No one has fucked me before, he types.

They feel immensely confident, despite having never done it, that they would know exactly how to do it.

i am still virgin and it is
way too big for me i
think but i was turned on by its pure and minimal design
:)

He sends a picture of the double dildo—silicone, black, wet—in his small hand.

> *you will need a coach to help*
> *you learn to take it like a good boy*

i did not want such a big
one but i don't like ugly stuff so i have chosen the only one
which is elegant and minimal
:)

A few weeks after this chat, Seasonal finds the dildo in the online store of a feminist sex shop in Amsterdam and orders it.

Chatting with strangers on the internet is like having a Tamagotchi, they think as they wander in concentric circles in Paris.

A few days into the visit, Seasonal walks alone from the hotel to the Père Lachaise Cemetery. Y and her daughter are hiding from the heat, but Seasonal wants to feel its threat, to be overwhelmed by it. It is thirty-six degrees by 10:00 a.m. The night before, they had started chatting with Odysseus on the hookup app.

They quickly leave the main path in the cemetery and walk over the uneven, hilly ground in the shade. It is silent and hot, and they are crying. Since H left, they have become accomplished at crying in public. A new skill, along with chatting with strangers on the internet, they are learning to relish.

Seasonal sits in the shade on the narrow path between the graves on the side of the hill and smokes, their wet face bringing some relief from the scorching air. A man in beige chinos and a white shirt asks them for directions to the grave of Chopin. They look it up on Google Maps and point him in what they hope is the right direction.

Eventually, in need of some kind of purpose, they decide to find Oscar Wilde's tomb. They had bought his collected works at nineteen and devoured them. Like so many readers before them, Seasonal wanted to live his boldness and lack of apology. At nineteen they had no idea what that would mean for them, what it would look like; they just knew it was a way to live.

They find Wilde toward the back of the cemetery and sit in the gutter opposite. They smoke and give it a long look. They watch people come and go. Seasonal observes that people tend to spend less than five minutes looking at the grave. Many of the people carry a laminated list of the famous dead in their hands or are accompanied by a guide.

Seasonal sits in the gutter for an hour watching the people who do not really seem to be looking at anything, watching the grave, listening to the heat.

They were not expecting Wilde's tomb to be so flamboyant. A large winged figure, carved by Jacob Epstein in 1914. *Of course it is flamboyant*, they think halfway through their third cigarette. The wings. The flat knees (*Was Oscar on his knees? Or did he like a boy who was?*). The long hands and feet. The Egyptian undertones.

Bees buzz in the trees overhead. Seasonal cannot see them.

They introjected that flamboyance at nineteen. Then they ignored it in order to try to make some kind of life for themself. Its wings appear to have grown.

Around 2:00 a.m. on their last night in Paris, unprompted, the Parisian sends a voice message saying *Oui, Madame*, and Seasonal feels like they have unlocked a new level of the game. A hard determination immediately takes hold of them: they must receive an audio file of him saying *Oui, Seasonal* before they leave Paris.

The Parisian sends the longed-for audio file as they are checking out of the hotel. They are standing in a black-tiled toilet stall when the message arrives and they tell him *there is room for you to kneel here*. He sends a text swoon.

Later, sitting on a crowded and airless Thalys, they send a goodbye text:

> *sorry we didn't get to meet,*
> *maybe next time.*

He responds and they keep flirting. He is working from home, naked because of the heat, and is, evidently, open to distraction. An hour into the trip he is lying on his bed trying to insert the black dildo into his anus and sending Seasonal blurry pictures.

They tell him to thank them, he sends a voice message: *Merci, Seasonal.*

A few hours later Seasonal is standing at the back of Amsterdam Centraal Station, smoking beside the IJ river while Y and her daughter drink tea in Starbucks.

sorry for the dirty pics
i was a bit under control
;)
the good thing is that i can
take it ;)
now i sure about it
softly and not too hardly

They smile and look out at the water, thinking about taking something *not too hardly.*

A few days later, the Parisian explains that he has a life philosophy as well as strong design philosophy.

i love mutants

people who are different

with superpowers

i hear a deep mystery

you are cold and warm

boy and girl

smart and animal

soft and tough

Seasonal is relearning, learning again and anew, the power of language. The Parisian calls them a *boyish girl* and they feel surprisingly seen. The next day he calls them *boy*.

I have never called a girl « boy »
but you make me think it
so badly

You are uncommon
That's your superpower
:)

Calling you « boy » is such
a great turn-on

Seasonal's self shifts on its axis. Their past and present realign. Their shaved head at twenty, the wide stance they would often adopt in photographs or when standing on the street, the steel-toe boots. When he calls them *boy*, new knowledge springs fully formed into them: They know exactly how to fuck a girl like him with their cock and until that moment—when he typed *boy*—they had no idea they knew how to. They are strong in their stance. They are the boy that turns him into a girl.

Is this interpellation? Am I what he sees, what he names? They sit on their grey felt couch, which they are sleeping on now they can no longer bear to lie next to H, who sits upstairs, ignoring them. *Why does it feel true, and how can it feel so true the moment he types it and it has never occurred to me? How does it come to the surface? Is it a coming to surface, or a contact with depth, a fantasy, or perhaps just an error of judgement? A projection?*

They are strong in their stance.

You are good to make others show
you their secrets

yes ;)
you were hoping i would know
what to do with you

Oui
How did you know?

The phone. Its curves, its thin body, its joyful metallic ping, its light and reassuring presence. Is the phone the stand-in for the body of the absent lover, or is the device itself the lover?

A few weeks later, Y and her daughter have returned to Australia, and the Russian brings a small yellow notebook to his first date with Seasonal. He sits it carefully on the edge of the table and tells them it contains a list of all the things they had agreed they wanted to talk about while chatting in the hookup app. Seasonal finds this list-making inexplicably endearing. He is small, fragile, with thin hair and big brown eyes.

"I am sorry," the Russian tells them over tea in a café with a tortoise-shell cat, *it is an emotion in English, but in Russian you say "Please forgive me" or "I am guilty." Russian is a language of shame.*

He has given up his passport and his citizenship. He says he will not go back.

He tells Seasonal they had him when he read *feminist* on their profile, because he does not think a woman should mother her male partner.

The conversation moves very quickly into emotional territory. The Russian is trying to avoid a mess. *We need to know how to deal with conflict. It is inevitable.* This sounds so true when said in a Russian accent. Seasonal believes him.

I will say things that trigger a reaction that is not about me but about your previous relationship. The same will happen for me. We need a stop word.

You mean a safe word? they ask.

Oh. Yes. He pauses.

Oh, you are not into BDSM, are you?

Seasonal compartmentalizes the slut and the Parisian and feigns a casual *no.*

H moves out. He goes to live with his mother in a small village thirty minutes from Utrecht. Seasonal wants to feel triumphant and free. And they do. They think the two of them might find their way back to each other—after all, plenty of people do. They want H to find his happiness as a monk. Having never been abandoned before, Seasonal does not recognize what has happened to them. It is only years later, when the pandemic comes, that they will realize what he had done.

On the next date, on the square outside the café, Seasonal kisses the Russian. It is tentative and exploratory. He is light and fragile. Is he dissolving into thin air as the kiss unfolds? The physical weightlessness of the Russian is in sharp contrast with his deep, resonant voice, which they find hypnotic. The hypnotism is enhanced by his innate command of narrative. He has a way of answering a question with a short story. Information comes through small details, events, progression, and context. His stories are always furnished with precisely enough description to make Seasonal feel they are entering a world. But it is the timbre of his voice that enacts this movement: a sonic transportation device.

When they compliment him on his story-answers, on their third date, he is surprised. His face is all skepticism and wariness.

No one likes my stories.

His colleagues joke about them, and he is accustomed to people interrupting him or asking him to get to the point. Seasonal asks if his children like his stories.

No, boys are not interested.

I like them. I could listen to them all day, they risk total honesty.

The strange word choices, so much stronger than a native English speaker … but as he speaks they can't hold on to the stories. Seasonal dissolves into the forest, the stones: the Russian standing there, looking at a clearing in the trees in the forest he has made with his words.

On their third date, the Russian says: *Remind me to tell you sometime about when the skinheads broke my nose.* And so, on their fourth date, sitting on their couch, he does.

The Russian and the Skinheads (a story-answer, recorded on Seasonal's iPhone)

Seasonal: So there were skinheads in your hometown, or did they *come* to your town?

The Russian: No, they were … they pretended to be … Well, it was rather simple, me and friend were walking across the central street of the town. The Red Street. It was called like that *red*, but in Russian, but it was red. And we had a bottle of beer in each of our hands, so I had a beer, he had a beer, we were just going by. It was … I think it was September, or October, but it was warm and dry and nice weather. And then, while we were passing by we heard some voices shouting. And oh, by the way, we both had longer hair, and the piercing … the earrings. And those guys shouted at us, and well, basically, they were looking for someone to chase. So they typically would go after anybody, any guys, with longer hair, trying to challenge them on being gay. But that was just really an excuse. So we didn't notice that somebody shouts, because it is a noisy street etcetera, but then when we realized that something's happening we were already attacked. And there were, like, I don't know, seven or something of those guys. And I think they were already on something like drugs. Really aggressive and energetic and stuff. So that's when it happened. Um … They attacked us, we tried to run away, we were surrounded. I crushed the bottle of beer which was in my hand to make kind of a sharp weapon, and that's when that guy jumped at me and hit my nose with his forehead.

And then we run away. And running, running, running, running, until we—I thought we were going into the inside court between the buildings that had another exit, but it didn't. So it was like dead end. So we ran inside, realized that there is nowhere to run further and the guys are after us, so we just run to some random door, knocked inside, frantically. It was open, they let us inside, closed the door afterward, called the police. While this crowd of people outside were ranting and raving and shouting and whatnot. The police came. Essentially they escorted us inside of their car, drove away, fast enough for those guys not to be able to run after, and then let us to go on our business. But eventually my nose was broken. And next morning, I made quite a show at my work … because you know … ever since my eyes have this bags under; I think there's some damage in circulation of, I don't know, blood or lymph or something. Then it was really, really … I had blue bags under my eyes and really swollen nose and everything and continued for, like, two weeks. I made into the stories of everybody around. But that was it. So broken nose. Skinheads. That's it.

The Russian lies in Seasonal's large bed in the dark. With C's help, they had dragged it into a different room after H had left. They are not used to sleeping in this part of the apartment, but they have already discovered that they can have sex in this room. The Russian is suspicious because he has always thought that happiness must come out of struggle: *If there is no struggle, is there life?* he asks earnestly.

Seasonal explains Lauren Berlant's theory of "cruel optimism": that we think struggle is necessary because the ideals of a good life are inherently punishing. The Russian listens, he likes that Seasonal appears to be smart. He reaches for their naked body.

A few days later Seasonal is stir-frying broccoli and making a move in the online Scrabble game they play with a friend in Australia. The Russian calls. His *soon-to-be ex-wife* has asked that he stop dating while she undergoes experimental marijuana treatment for the breast cancer she does not want to treat with traditional methods. Seasonal saw it coming, this moment. From everything he had said over the month they were getting to know each other better. They understand, and let the Russian go.

Echoing in their ears is something he said during one of their marathon dates: *I want to get off the needle of not being good enough.* Months later, when they want to remember his phrasing of this striking statement, they try to see if he said it in iMessage. But the app has no search function, and so they will never know. They cannot bring themself to scroll through the thousands of texts they exchanged. But checking for the search function, they inadvertently see the furtive selfies he sent them. The last one he sent, he almost got it right—he almost looked through the camera to them, to show them the face they saw on their couch when he was telling them about the skinheads.

A few days after this phone call in which he says it has to end, they have the kind of sex with the Russian that Seasonal thought no longer existed. Their molecules are rearranged. They are the dynamic flow of matter, the *zoē*. They can retain a sense of this state for at least a day afterward, and they go off to Berlin to meet a friend thinking *YES*.

These men from the eastern part of Europe with deep baritone voices. They speak slowly, with strong, unfamiliar rhythms. The sound is unbelievably erotic. These men could say anything to them and Seasonal would listen. They realize now that they have always found the high-pitched nasal sound of Australian men speaking grating.

Somewhere between that first phone call trying to end it and the actual end, the Russian calls late one night. Panic stains his voice and he is speaking in staccato. His wife claims to have found out Seasonal's identity, and she is threatening to have them killed by thugs from Chechnya. She has screamed at him that she knows that Seasonal has been prescribed antidepressants (they haven't) and that two years ago they had an abortion (they didn't).

They listen as he pours his panic down the phone. Clearly he is in an emotionally abusive relationship. They will not validate the threat by taking it seriously, but they want to take the Russian's emotional response seriously because they like him, and they want to help him.

They talk him down as best they can.

And as they fall asleep they imagine themself as Jason Bourne: opening the door to their office at the university to find a cluster of pale, balding men in black vinyl jackets with stony faces and no visible weapons.

They know an Australian associate professor in the faculty of humanities killed by hitmen in the provincial city of Utrecht would not make it past the first full draft of the script.

Seasonal is starting conversations with strangers trying to see what the world has to say to them, trying to discover their contents by inviting others to look into them. They are discovering the world has a lot to say: about desire as a drive, a driver, an excess, a longing that demands to be filled. People say *hello* to each other and the demands begin: dominate me, fuck me, give me a sense of novelty, confirm to me that I exist and that you see me. Confirm to me that an intelligent woman will take me seriously, will let me talk, will not take my cock-mind in her hand and laugh, will not (worse still) turn away in boredom or disgust.

This is the attention economy of online dating: raw, fundamental desires to be seen and to see, to have a sense of possibility, and to be authorized to fantasize.

As the summer fades, Seasonal is aflame with the desire to bring these fantasies into reality. But they are also trying to contend with the shame and shock of what trying to hold on to their desire has demanded. They are truly alone, and truly foreign.

Seasonal feels the summer slipping away. They begin to dread the return of the darkness and the northerly wind. They meet the Sound Engineer, whom they have not seen in several months.

There are three forms of fighting in aikido, he tells them as they drive away from the restaurant he had chosen in a city to the east of the Netherlands, where he feels confident none of his friends will see him out with someone who is not his partner. Despite being an ethical nonmonogamist, none of his friends know he is bisexual or in an open relationship.

There is power to power, but you can always lose, there is always someone stronger than you. You can attack the structure of their stance so they cannot deploy their power. And you can pull them out of their zone of power.

Seasonal finds all his talk about aikido deeply interesting but they also wonder if it is a kind of defense in itself.

They sit together in a comfortable silence, and then the Sound Engineer says confidently, *I know what you should research next.*

Seasonal is amused. *Oh, really? Tell me.*

The Dark Web. I would love to know what someone like you would make of the Dark Web.

They were ready to mock him, but they have to admit this is a good idea.

Later, after sex, they stand smoking together on the balcony of Seasonal's apartment. He turns to them and with admiration in his voice tells them:

You can really take a beating and enjoy it.

They laugh.

The New Violence

Hello dear S,

*i write because of the exceptionally
high matching score. nice to know that
I'm not alone. :)
L*

It is autumn when László sends his introductory message on the app. Seasonal is gripping on to their job while their life falls apart in a foreign country. They are not sure that talking to the world in this state is a good idea, but they don't know what else to do while they are in free fall. They try to trust that this breaking apart is also a coming together.

László is very attracted to women with short hair, and immediately after making contact in the app he asks them about their haircut— *Is it a statement of some kind?* Seasonal answers, *I just feel more like myself with short hair,* and then they hit the ball back over the net while standing in line at the bakery:

> *is your interest in kink an interest in exploring or engaging power as a political/ social force, or do you tend to think of it as (purely?) erotic?*

I don't think the two can exist separately. There is no such thing as purely erotic, at least not in sex.

I have a number
of things I'm
trying to explore with
BDSM.

Playing with power,
releasing it from its
ossified state, liquidating
it, so it can
be communicated,
exchanged, played,
experimented with, is
what I do in
kink. It gives me
great pleasure to
be free.

May I ask why
did you ask
this question? It
was no ordinary question.

And I want to
tell you: your
question turned me on.

Later that evening, Seasonal cradles the phone and types the answer
they hope they are capable of:

hi lászló, i really
liked your answer
a lot: the idea
of releasing power
from its ossified
state (beautifully put)
but also how bringing
it to the fore
makes it available
to be exchanged and
played with. i
am very interested
in this aspect of
kink too.

what made me ask?

well, you are one
of the few people
who signaled their
interest in bdsm
in their profile in
a way that
made me think you
had thought about it.
seems i was right
:)

*i have also had
a lot of conversations
with people—
especially recently—
around kink.
it is very interesting
to me on all
levels (intellectually,
interpersonally, erotically,
etc.). i am
particularly interested
in how dominance/
submission can work
as a crosscurrent
in gendered forms
of power.*

*and how nice that
my question turned
you on . . .
an added bonus :)*

*yes, it's a turn-
on, because it
opens up so many
possibilities.*

that start with
whether we speak
about this

and then, if
yes, how

and how speech turns
into phisical *physical

and, as you
say, how gender
relations shade this.

I have played with
men, and there
power exchange was
purely that, if you
like a reversal to
the pack-hierarchy
state of affairs among
competing males. very
pre-cognitive, and
proto-social.

playing with women,
for me, is a
much richer experience,
because the contemporary
politics of gender is
always part of the
play, whether we
know it / or
want it, or reflect
on it.

and the cuts, bruises,
and rope marks
don't just stay on
the skin, or the
soul, but also
on the body politic.

may i ask what
you are into?

"i am a novice
with a calling,"
would be the
short answer.

I have so many
things to say,
but I would
like to say it
in person.

If you feel
comfortable with the
idea, I'd love to
meet you.

Despite this profession of enthusiasm, László finds it hard to find the energy to open his calendar. It takes two weeks of chatting. When he finally admits he is free, Seasonal suggests they meet at the café in the film museum in Amsterdam, which sits on an island behind Centraal Station and has a beautiful view of the IJ river and the city.

On the ferry to meet László on a chilly fall afternoon, Seasonal is terrified. They stand wide-legged amongst the tourists, scooters, and the bicycles and type frantically into their phone:

I am trying to inhabit my dom self: my stance, open body language, standing in my power, practicing my dismissive/assessing gaze: looking forward to the game. Hoping I can play it, that I am able to play, that he is willing.

What does it mean to try to bring fantasy into reality? To try to bend the world to your will, to find a part of the world that wants to be bent? To punish, to instruct, to immobilize, to make the other wait, to hold their reality within yours?

László has not chosen a table. He is standing in the atrium between the café and the stairs to the cinemas. He is tall, his skin the color of roasted almonds. They greet each other with shy smiles and go in search of a table. The raised section at the back of the café is quiet, but each table has a sign that reads *Gereserveerd*. While pretending to look for a table, Seasonal sounds out the Dutch pronunciation in their mind, as it has the strong guttural *g* they are still learning to mediate. *Ge-res-er-veert. Have to remember to say the* d *as* t, they think, as they wonder *Who made all these reservations and where the hell are they?* Eventually they agree with László on a spot on a long bench facing the water. László dismissively moves the "Reserved" sign in a swift, fluid movement. This gesture speaks volumes about his attitude to authority. It seals the deal: the muscles in their pelvis pulse with wanting.

The two of them sit side by side on the bench overlooking the IJ. They talk ideas for the first hour. He is from Budapest and researches the internet. He asks them about the book they are finishing, and wants a chapter-by-chapter description. Seasonal dutifully gives one. They do not know how to shift out of this very familiar persona of the affable humanities researcher explaining their work. While they talk their book their mind is frantically trying to find the door that allows them to be something else—the thing they've come here to try to be.

They are immensely relieved but also disappointed with themself when László finally introduces the topic of their shared interest in kink. Seasonal pushes themself to be honest about everything, but also painfully struggles to translate the low throbbing in their body, the high energy of excitement, the recent explosion in their erotic imagination. How to elucidate the strange feeling that even though they have had practically no experience (knowingly) inflicting pain and dominating the other, they are going to be really good at it? They push through their sense of unease about appearing ridiculous or inexperienced; they know enough to know that a dom cannot be self-conscious. It is one of the many things they like about the headspace.

After two hours, Seasonal has to leave. They have scheduled another meeting as an insurance policy against László being boring. He asks if he can walk with them some of the way in a hopeful and soft voice that he has not used in the last two hours. His posture is still tall, but Seasonal senses how hope changes his bearing. His familiarity to them in this moment is disorienting. They know exactly what they are seeing.

As they leave the café they lie and tell László that they are teasing a sub they know that he would be replaced if this date went well. He says nothing and looks straight ahead. As they approach the wooden stairs that lead down to the footpath, he looks down. His voice is quiet, deep, and without the boldness that has characterized its timbre up until this moment.

I would like that.

Their whole body responds to this meagre wish. Certainty plumps their clitoris and the soft gel discs between their vertebrae. Their stride lengthens just a little.

Later, a message arrives:

We talked Foucault, but
the subtext was
something more visceral.

I was trying to
get a glimpse
of how your eyes
glitter when cruel,
when greedy, when they deny.

We exchanged ideas
but my painful
awareness of your
scent made me think
of exchanging body
fluids.

The next day Seasonal can barely remember anything about the interaction with László: it is a blur of sense memory. The tarnished light on the water, the low hum of their desire growing louder and more insistent. The way his eyes moved. They could feel him reacting to them. But they cannot remember anything about him: Brown hair? A black T-shirt with thin white stripes under a black cardigan? Blue jeans? The cardigan was fastened by a red plastic brooch that said *Alarm*. He wore a ring. Three black plastic disks joined by wire, each with white numbers from zero to ten. Which finger? And glasses … does he wear glasses? They cannot remember. Their ability to encode memory was weakened by the cognitive and corporeal task of processing the light, the water, how far they were from home, how far from their friends, how wonderful it was to be there then talking to a stranger about the games they could play to release power from its ossified state.

They start chatting with László every day via WhatsApp, and the following Monday he flies to South Korea to attend a conference as a keynote speaker. The negotiations of the terms of his surrender begin in earnest.

You have a very
rich and deep
sensuality

So exciting and
unique

And so very private

At least so it
seems

I feel very lucky
that you shared
some of it with
me

I just wanted
to thank you
for this

I wanted you
to know that I
appreciate the value
of it

László likes to send Seasonal erotic photographs of male submission. The subject's face is rarely visible in these images, and so the opening move in the game they want to play with him while he travels to Seoul is to request an airport selfie. The aim of the game is for him to learn proper forms of address in submission. In response to the request for a selfie, he sends three nicely framed arty shots of the airport in which his reflection or shadow is barely visible.

> *you are bad at*
> *selfies, i suspect,*
> *because you do*
> *not want to be*
> *seen.*

> *you are going to*
> *have to try again.*
> *look through the*
> *camera in your*
> *phone and let me*
> *see you.*

> *this is the first*
> *lesson in how*
> *to address me.*

> *i am waiting.*

They assign a custom tone (Glass) to László in WhatsApp. The two short rings of the glass serve two purposes: their pleasure (giving him a distinct sonic presence amongst the stream of notifications they receive), and the omnipresence of the dom. They will allow this tone to interrupt them so that László may experience them as a near-constant presence.

Before he boards the plane to Seoul, László asks:

*Do I sense correctly
that you have a
specific interest in
power over the male
(body?), not just
simply the other, or
the body?*

yes

*What is the role
of gender? Or sex?*

*they both have a
role. would you
like me to elaborate?*

Negotiations with László continue after he arrives in Seoul. Seasonal lies naked in bed, and the chat with him is rapid:

what do you fear?

I fear that you
might order me to
do something that is
not entirely appropriate

And demand proof
that I obeyed

are you afraid i
will force your
submissive and quotidian
states together?

I refuse to answer
that question

oh?
will you tell me
why?

With your permission,
I prefer not to
tell you why

oh, you are tired
from your flight
and you feel unsafe.

it is so impossible
to read this
situation: i wish
you were in the
room with me and
i could use all
my senses to
read you now.

:)

I do fear the
collapse of the
submissive and
the quotidian

Seasonal is happy they were able to guide him through his fear. They understand his fear of being ensnared by desire. They sign off the chat by agreeing neither of them will masturbate, they will each hold on to the erotic tension that is building and bring it to their next meeting. Seasonal puts the phone down and breaks the promise immediately—they know, somehow, that this is what the dom should do. Seek their own pleasure.

I'll send you a
black heart every
time you shake my
core in a way
that I'm happy to
explore further despite
of, or exactly
because of, my feelings.

The next morning Seasonal messages with László in Seoul, and then rides their large Omafiets to class. He sends them a teasing message that pushes them into the classroom feeling flighty and too charged for the pedagogical scene. They tell him he needs to get better at pleasing, not just teasing . He offers to make it up to them.

Tell me when you
are alone.

                                                        almost home

I'll be waiting here.
What is your desire,
should I write or
speak to you?

                                                              omg
                                                  you will speak
                                                          to me?

Do you want
me to?

                                                              fuck
                                                               yes

I'm grateful for
you letting me
try to please you.

You have beautiful sounding orgasms, László says over a WhatsApp voice connection from South Korea.

i want you to
know i have no
interest in abuse.

What constitutes abuse
does not entirely
depend on you.

oh, i know that
there is a long
story there

i have to find
a way to confront
my fear about the
inevitable relationship
between power and
abuse and that means
running the risk
that you will feel
abused by me
and i have to
believe that you will
tell me if that
happens and that
you will forgive
me for it.

The sooner you tell
me, the better.

i grew up in
a physically and
emotionally abusive
house but i am
ok :)
but it has left
me with questions
about gender and power,
because it was my
father (unsurprisingly)
who was abusive
and i am a lot
like my father
in many ways.
some of the best
parts of me come
from him.

(i am worried
you are going to
walk out of
this arrangement now.)

so i need to
make it clear
that when i see
men, i do not
see my father.
i see my father
in myself.

but it is not
him, actually,
that i see.
i have moved
a great distance
(emotionally and
physically) from
him and the
house i grew
up in.

but on the few
occasions when i
have genuinely felt
my will to power,
i have immediately
turned from it and
denied it.

And then comes the gift Seasonal was not expecting:

I hope I can
help you find
your own voice
of power.

A few days later, Seasonal lies in bed and types into their phone in the dim morning light. They ask László if he will let them use his body and his sexuality so that they can relearn the association between pain and pleasure. They hope that by understanding how pain and pleasure come together for him, they can find out what kind of pain they might like to give. When they ask him, he fails to answer correctly; he does not give Seasonal the *yes* they want.

I appreciate you
asking my permission,
but is that really
necessary?

try again.

May I ask why
do you ask my
permission to give
pain?

read my request
again.

May I ask why
do you think your
request isn't covered
by my submission
to your will?

And so they must administer the first punishment.

It comes to them fully formed, and their heart races. They know it must involve the senses, that they must shock the body and create a situation that forces him to reflect. They tell him to text them when he is back in his hotel room and they will tell him what his punishment is. He sends the black heart emoji in response.

In the hours while they wait for him to text from Seoul, they mark book reviews written by their students, they take a walk, they eat muesli and Greek yoghurt. They refine their strategy. They know they cannot write the instructions out and have them ready to cut and paste into the app when he contacts them. They have to type them in real time so that he has the experience of seeing the *typing* cue and the sense of anticipation can build. He needs to feel them instructing him; the time it takes for them to type the instructions feeds the pleasure and fear of anticipation.

They leave the apartment, desperate to stretch their legs. They walk their usual route through a nature reserve, past several canals and some garden plots, then back through their neighborhood. Seasonal notices none of these things. They are composing and practicing their lines. Their sense of ruthlessness swells, their gait becomes longer and their feet hit the pavement with decisiveness. Their torso is a chamber that holds a pristine and unfathomable power. Their body language is open and they are longing for László.

Finally, the two sharp sounds ring out from their pocket.

I'm here.
I would like to
know what I
did wrong.

the punishment will
help you find that
out.

They are ready. But when they realize it is their moment, their palms are wet and their blood is thumping in their ears. The membrane separating fantasy from reality is as thin as the iPhone into which they attempt to pour their dominance. Before they begin to type their lines, they think, *Am I really about to punish a man I am attracted to, whom I have met once, who is eight and a half thousand kilometers away?*

They sit on their couch and start typing.

i have a timer
set on my phone.
you can set one
too. set it for
an hour.

then do the
following:

1. use the word-
search function in
WhatsApp on our

chat and search
the word "yes"

2. scroll through
the results

3. take a cold
shower

4. lie naked, face
down, wet, on the
tiled floor of your
bathroom for thirty
minutes

5. call me and
tell me what you
have learned about
submission.

I understand, and
do as you say.

Seasonal opens the door to their balcony, and they light a cigarette. Their hand is shaking. The timer is running. They feel something new, hard, exciting in their chest.

László calls them after he has gotten up from the floor. They ask him what he has learned. He says he learned that he does not say *yes* very often. When they ask why that is, he tells them:

I will do anything to avoid saying yes. I fear if I say yes there is no room for my opinion.

They ask how he felt lying on the bathroom floor.

I felt alone.

He tells them he went into himself and concentrated on his breath. He came up off the floor feeling stronger.

Do you understand now, Seasonal asks forcefully, voice shaking, *what I can give you?*

Yes.
They ask if he thinks the strength he feels now will wear off.

No, it is part of me now. I lay, wet, on the floor because a stranger thousands of miles away told me to. That is a unique experience. I will not forget it.

How do you feel about me now? they ask, curious, afraid, alive with a new timbre of curiosity.

Lucky to be your play pal.

Seasonal wonders if László would say *yes* more easily if they knew the pleasure it brings them. He wants to be an instrument of their pleasure, and they shook his core in an earlier chat when they told him that when they use him for their pleasure they will not care about how he feels or about his pleasure.

Shall I tell you what your "yes" means to me?

If you think it will help me understand.

They tell him that his *yes* brings them a new, and great, form of satisfaction. That submission does not happen once, it happens over and over again and the *yes* is just as important as whatever it is he is agreeing to do for them. The *yes* is his submission. The *yes* is their prize.

They tell him that in submission his opinion does not matter—that is why he needs to learn to say *yes*. To realize he is irrelevant. What matters is that he submits, that he says it.

In the space of twenty-four hours, he says after this lecture on the "yes," *you have made me come and made me lie wet on the floor for thirty minutes. A few more like this and I will think you are some kind of James Bond villain.*

This is music, this is a kind of sexual pleasure Seasonal had no idea existed.

Seasonal rereads their question to László over the voice connection. They want to know if he can say *yes* this time. They sit on the couch and read the text aloud:

there is a gap
between my desire
and my capacities
that i think you
can help me cross,
and it relates
to physical pain
this in turn affects
my ability to
administer punishment,
which i have
already told you
i am interested
in exploring ;)

i think to
overcome this, i
want to learn
more about the
pain that brings
you pleasure in
order to learn
how they go
together for you.

the idea of
giving you the
pain that you
want fills me
with desire.

and i want to
use that desire
to reorder the
associations i
have learned.

in that reordering,
i hope to discover
which forms of pain
i like to give.

can you give me
this opportunity,
lászló?

Without a pause, he says into the phone:

Yes.

It is Seasonal's first victory.

They are metal filings responding to a new magnetic force, pulled violently across the surface of their previous assumptions about the forms desire will take.

Somewhere in this haze, Seasonal wonders where all this knowledge came from, and why they feel so certain in it.

When Seasonal tells Y what László's punishment was, she laughs hard and long and says, *Seasonal, it is like performance art.*

When they tell Q what László's punishment was, he says, *You should make him read you Foucault and flog him every time he mispronounces a word.*

When they tell C what László's punishment was, and that he felt stronger when he got up off the floor, she says, *Wow. It is like a form of therapy.*

They tell M via recorded message in WhatsApp that they are practicing BDSM. She responds by asking *What exactly does it mean for you to be dominant?*

I could Google all this, obviously, she says in her voice message, *but I want you to tell me. What does it mean that you dom him?*

Once he has returned to Amsterdam from South Korea, arranging a second date with László is tricky business. He has said he lives with a woman, they have a son, and they have an open relationship. On the app he listed himself as single. They pause briefly to consider what these deceits might mean, but then dismiss them as irrelevant. They are not interested in thinking about László as a person, and so his capacity for honesty is not an issue. The revelation of his family life has a more immediate impact: as a person with no children, Seasonal is invariably drawn into the logistics of parenting when dating parents. László has to arrange a sleepover for his son in order to be able to see them, and so the social arrangements of a ten-year-old child become entangled in their play. The mindset they adopt when talking about this is to be as easygoing as possible, but every time they have to listen to the practicalities—from László, the Sound Engineer, or the Russian—they think *Imagine how much harder this must be for the woman.*

A day later László informs Seasonal that his son does indeed have a sleepover. They feel sick to their stomach. Their bowels clench. They wonder how on earth they can inhabit space with him.

They suggest via text message that they meet him at the train station and that they take a walk.

Would it be possible
to meet somewhere
less stressful and
transitory?

He is so far from submission. After some gentle teasing, they compromise.

This is what Seasonal does every day. Give way when they can tell someone needs something more than they do. They like to do it. They are trying to like it less.

As they negotiate their meeting, László proposes he devise a symbolic way of registering his submission to them—he will give them something before he enters their house that symbolizes his submission. As they walk through the streets of Utrecht after eating ramen, they are like any other pair on the street enjoying the relatively calm, cold weather of late autumn. At the door to their apartment, László pauses and says,

I must give you this before I enter, and hands them a piece of rope.

It is beautifully rolled, and held together by a simple knot. They know László uses rope—he has mentioned in a chat that time unfolded differently *the last time I was tied*, and that *I can be abusive when I rope top*. The rope is rough; it would hurt like hell if it was tied right. Seasonal is terrible at knots—a rebellion against being sent to Brownies and then Girl Guides when they really wanted to be in Boy Scouts (*where the uniforms were so much better*). They take the rope, and thank him, and feel its weight in their hand. He has a great poker face, until he gives in to his desire, and then everything is written there. But for now, they can only admire his solemnity and care, and the attentive beauty in the way he has tied the rope to itself.

Seasonal invites him in and makes some tea. Shortly afterward, László stands on the balcony watching Seasonal smoke and explains how much he likes the Enlightenment. He thinks it has bequeathed Us a lot of Good Things, like Rationality, and Choice, and Autonomy.

Seasonal doesn't know where to start in response, but later in the evening when he puts their hand on his scrotum and asks them to squeeze and says *Don't be afraid*, they squeeze harder than they ever thought they would dare.

Seasonal redirects the conversation by inviting him back inside. They open a drawer in the small bookcase and give him what he had asked for: a symbol he can use to signal his submission to their will. They hand him a brand new MAC Cosmetics kohl eyeliner. He is perplexed.

You have to write it on your body, they tell him. *I have chosen something ephemeral: it will wear off, and you will have to renew it.*

His eyes expand. He pauses to think. He likes it. They knew he would.

Not long after being given the eyeliner, he takes the lid off the pencil and draws a small black heart on the soft inside of his left wrist. Their will to master swells: they knew he would do this too. This is the emoji he sends in their chats when they have shaken his core. When László finally asks for permission to kiss them, after hours of talking and drinking tea and wearing his mark of submission on his wrist sitting on their couch, he comes to their body tentatively and then like a thunder clap. They lie beneath him, he rises above them on his elbows and knees. Every muscle in his body, all his senses, and his mind are engaged. He stares at them, smells them, kisses their mouth their face their neck, he is greedy and fast, but then something quieter rolls in, impressively tender and light. Seasonal thinks he has a physical range like Freddie Mercury's rumored four octaves—and he likes to use them all.

When he slides his finger along their edge on this, their second, meeting, Seasonal signals their assent to everything, to whatever is coming, with a quiet hum. He lifts his lips from their neck to their ear and whispers:

I remember that sound.

They lead him upstairs. They undress and are lost in exploring each other.

If you like pain, you can give it, László tells them in the dim light of their bedroom. *Where do you like it? Show me on my body.*

Seasonal has no words. They are being rearranged, and they have lost their edges. They wrest the language center of their brain into action.

I can't. How can I show you when your body is different from mine?

He puts his hand between their legs.

Here. This. This is the only thing I don't have. Is this where you like to feel pain?

They are lost in the touch. Firm. Concentrated. A grip.

After rearranging them this way, they lie facing each other. László tells them he thinks they have similar pain thresholds. They have no idea what this means. He guides their hand to his scrotum.

Here. Give me pain here.

They feel a pulse of resistance, of fear, of incredulity. But his large hand, encircling theirs, is firm, and they trust him. They take his soft scrotum in their hand and find his testicles. The small glands slip about under their grip, the sack way larger than the items it carries. They gently coax one into their palm. They lie on top of László's warm body—with its even dark complexion which they find so charming—and they squeeze.

Go for it, he says. *Don't be afraid.*

When pain arrives during the heightened state of sexual arousal, it brings new colors, new sounds, new forms of pressure and response. Unheralded possibilities materialize for why two bodies might seek each other, and how two bodies might be used to alter the structures of feeling and thinking in the minds they carry. The sharp-thirsty lust of desire without pain—desire that does not call out to pain—is transmogrified. No longer the limit case of intensity, its familiar rhythms are disrupted and reorganized. László takes the whole of Seasonal's labia in his right hand and makes it the focal point of everything the two of them have dared to think might be possible in the hundreds of messages they have exchanged. This is not a caress. Gripped this way—by Him, Now, Here—they recognize the cognitive load of deep learning. They know it from the years they spent studying *Bodies That Matter*, *The Dialectic of Sex*, *Beloved*, psychopaths, and ethics as an undergraduate; the intense mornings during their doctoral study as they waded through libraries and archives of self-published literature; from two years ago when they spent their sabbatical reading book history and media theory. This time the eyes and the brain are not the leaders—their cunt, their sphincter, their breasts, their mouth, their fingers, their ears, and their gut are leading this expedition, and these receptors are jubilant at the prospect that their time at the helm has arrived.

And there is the trust, the exposure, the extremely delicate balance of respect that makes pain a tool for learning and not for punishment. Seasonal has no understanding of how they have managed to build this with László so quickly, but they are reassured when they look at him across the white expanse of their too-big bed and see the awe they feel is mirrored in his face.

By the time they admit their exhaustion at 3:30 a.m., he falls asleep quickly. László snores. Seasonal lies awake beside his sleeping form. Muscles aching, brain fizzing, sleep will not come.

They wake when the first bird announces the feeble autumn dawn. They go to the bathroom. They are dehydrated from all the sweating and sighing. They brush their teeth, drink several glasses of water, and empty their bladder. They return to bed and László is snoring still.

But he also hums and sighs, and these sounds make a soundscape they are not opposed to. The snoring comes and goes, but the sound of his breathing is always expressive. He is a musical sleeper.

In the morning, they doze, and then Seasonal admits defeat and announces they will be making tea. László's head peeks out of the covers, and in response to their *do you want anything?* he says he *does not need anything*. They get out of bed and as they pass his feet on the way to the door they lift the covers and inspect them. They are the same beautiful even deep color as the rest of his body, but a little lighter in tone. And there is the heart he drew to mark his submission at some point deep in the night, when the mark on his wrist had disappeared through the friction of their attraction. They sit naked on the end of the bed and hold his foot in their hand. They like its weight. They lick their thumb and begin to rub the mark from his foot.

What are you doing? he cannot hide his incredulity.

I am removing the mark. It is from last night.

But it is not yours to remove.

It is, they declare. *You will have to mark yourself again if you want to continue to submit to me.*

They rub at the sole of his foot. The kohl is deep into the coarser (but remarkably soft) skin in the foot's arch. The mark does not leave easily, but after some rubbing and some more saliva and smiling they have reduced it to a smudgy shadow.

László looks confused and pleased from under the covers. Before they leave to make tea, they ask again:

Do you need anything?

Just a hot shower.

You have me confused. His face hovering above them, their tired, naked bodies touching and firing in the soft morning light. *I thought to submit to a feminist interested in disrupting gender roles would mean that I would have to deny my sexuality, my desire. I am not sure if it is right that I am here, on top, between your open legs.*

They laugh.

I cannot help you with this confusion. I am sorry.

He gets the joke, but also the meaning: they are here to confuse him.

You will have to stay confused by the fact that I want your desire. I want you where you are.

That is what is powerful about the pencil. When I drew the mark on my foot, I knew that I was free. I was free to express myself, and could rely on you to guide me.

Dominance is the weightless height of helium—their chest cavity a balloon, Seasonal's body is lifting above the scene. Transcendent.

From somewhere below, László tells them that their *intimacy* feels entirely different than he expected. He was expecting more struggle, to be taken further away from his desire, not deeper into it. Seasonal does not say anything; their brain flooded with hormones, they are beyond speech. But they feel somewhere that this is how they know he wants to submit. He finds freedom where he expected to feel constrained. Where he expected to be resisting.

Later, they sit on the dark-grey couch facing each other. Their eyes are warm with smiling. Their bodies point at each other, but like in the meeting at the film museum, they do not touch. They try to account for the algorithm. How did it know their perversions would be so compatible? The conversation flows, they are two minds making one question, one scene of interpretation. It is not an exchange; they join their inquiry together. This is what they will do with their bodies later—when they take turns mapping each other's thresholds, finding the coordinates of edges and pressure points, pausing on them to allow the other to feel their contours are being observed, then finding ways in, being inside and outside, each wanting a sensation of being the object of inquiry and the explorer. Not knowing which position they enjoy more. Knowing the pleasure is in being both. After some calm silence, László changes the subject:

What made you interested in a power exchange that reflects on gender?

Seasonal tries to explain how being socialized as a woman, into femininity, means that their sense of self-worth comes from accommodating other people. They are trying to learn how to move in the world differently, with less of a self-sacrificing disposition.

It is still a choice you make, to accommodate others. Why is it so hard? You have already made so many choices away from the standard.

They try to explain the cost of those choices away from the "standard," that the choices themselves—when and if they have been able to make them—work against their internalized sense of what it means to be a good person. Even though they recognize that this is the work of the patriarchy, it doesn't make violating their own sense of what it means to be a good person any easier. The patriarchy's ideas about a woman's worth as being located in her ability to make others happy, to give them what they need and desire (preferably without them asking for it), is theirs too. They pride themself on it, in their teaching, their friendships, their relationships with lovers. It is a perennial bulb that sits deep within their ego, their identity, their ego-ideal. Seasonal is hoping that a power exchange with László will help them locate this bulb, maybe, if he does not get bored or if they do not lose their nerve, so that they can uproot it.

This is what the Parisian releases them from when he calls them *boy*.

All choices come with a cost, László tells them confidently, his long frame stretching out on the couch as Seasonal gets up to make more tea.

Yes, but not all costs are equal, they counter.

That is irrelevant. The cost is paid nonetheless. My decision to leave Hungary, to refuse to live in a fascist state, has cost me dearly. But I am angry with the people I know who have not left. They would rather stay and be comfortable … they avoid adjusting to a new culture, a new language, a new way of living, and so they live in a fascist dictatorship.

They look at him on the couch and wonder what an Australian feminist and a married man from Hungary could have to say to each other. Each of them knows the intimate workings of Empire, and each chose to leave. Seasonal is from a country that burns, László is from a country that freezes. What does that have to do with what they're doing now?

I wrote a letter when I left, he says, looking out onto the row of small houses behind Seasonal's apartment. His open face clouds over.

I sent it to everyone I knew, telling them exactly why I left, telling them I would not be returning.

Seasonal does not know what to say to him. They sit still. A chasm of experience and knowledge is opening. It had never occurred to Seasonal that a person would know they were going into exile, but the moment they think this they realize *of course they can.* Seasonal tries to imagine what kinds of sentences a letter like the one László wrote would have. What it would say, to whom would he be speaking? Just as he taught them something with his body the night before, Seasonal's instincts tell them that László is now teaching them something else about pain.

The morning unfolds quietly toward midday.

Seasonal offers to walk László to the train station. This early in the afternoon, they already notice, the light is becoming paler, the days shorter. After walking a few blocks in silence, Seasonal offers an observation:

I like the way you bend time. I like the way time bends.

He is silent and keeps walking. He is thinking.

I have not thought of it this way before. I have not heard someone say it this way. I like it.

They arrive at the station after a short walk through the old inner city of Utrecht. They stand together quietly, looking at each other.

I am not good at this part, Seasonal says, with no trace of their dominance available.

See you next time, maybe, is his response.

They think they detect a smirk, but they are so tired they cannot tell. He brings his face close and brushes his cheek against theirs. They can smell their cunt on his face.

See you next time, maybe, they echo faintly.

They walk in opposite directions.

The next day Seasonal sends a message:

> *as the most*
> *tenuous traces of*
> *your presence in*
> *my apartment fade—*
> *the sense of how*
> *the rooms felt*
> *with you in them,*
> *the pleasure i*
> *took in watching*
> *& feeling you*
> *occupy space, your*
> *smell in my bed—*

i am enjoying
reading the constellation
of objects you left
behind:
the flowers (kangaroo
paw), the comic,
the rope (so
beautifully tied),
your toothbrush,
the mark of your
orgasm on my bed
cover.

together, and in
different combinations,
these objects point
in many directions.

A crime scene, where
from all these
signs, the keen
observer has the
chance to reconstruct
the future,
and not what has
already taken place.

Seasonal begins writing sentences and thinking thoughts they never thought possible. They are worried there is not enough time. That they will lose him before they have had a chance to destroy him. They want to give László the pleasure of being nothing. The more they come to like him, to value his sensitivity, his sharp mind, his aesthetics, his ethics, and the more they want his respect, the easier it seems to become to think about destroying him. By hand they wash the bed cover, removing the stain in hopeful anticipation that the opportunity might arise to make another.

In the following weeks, László sends them images of his body marked with the pencil. The black heart on his chest, on his thigh, *I submit to you* scrawled up the inside of his forearm. He is clearly enjoying exploring the possibilities it presents. Seasonal finds this autonomous use of the pencil and the mark for his own pleasure outrageous and delicious. How dare he write on himself with the tool they gave him so he could serve their pleasure? They think his desire is selfish. They realize they are quickly being absorbed into László's psychic world, and it unnerves them. To try to regain control of the situation, Seasonal asks László to meet them for a walk. He agrees, and they spend an hour walking along the Amstel River, and Seasonal is confident they have reestablished control. But as they board the train to return to Utrecht, a message arrives:

I also wore your
mark when we
met today.

A hot itch of irritation runs across Seasonal's body.

fatal mistake

Now I realize.

the mark means
nothing if i
do not see it.

it means less
than nothing.

(123)

it is insulting
to me, within
the power exchange
and outside it.

for the first time
it makes me think
that you are here
only for yourself.

Please go on.

i have nothing
else to say. you
changed the game,
i think.

i am tired.

A week later, Seasonal flies to Florence to meet an Australian friend, her husband, and their six-year-old daughter in Prato. The morning of their departure, they snap awake at 5:00 a.m. By the time they arrive in Florence at 12:30 p.m., they are exhausted. They are staying one night in an apartment in a medieval tower opposite the Uffizi Gallery: there is a large picture window that looks up the Arno River. The balcony where they smoke provides a view of the Cathedral of Santa Maria del Fiore—she towers ostentatiously above the terracotta-tiled roofs. Seasonal watches the shadows chased by the afternoon sun on the roofs around them, the autumn light holds a trace of summer heat.

They have been in Florence twice before but have never looked at frescoes. They walk to the Basilica of Santa Maria Novella. Despite being raised by committed atheists, in the last few years Seasonal has discovered a deep and inexplicable love of Gothic art. Painting before perspective, with rudimentary light and crazy, off-kilter ratios: tiny children and sheep, horses too large and dozens of flat human bodies layered on top of each other to make crowd scenes. They discovered this inexplicable love of flat people in the Uffizi Gallery on their first trip to Florence, with H. They had come here to celebrate the beginning of their fortieth year. They had bought timed tickets for the Uffizi and arrived at 8:00 a.m. H had sped off to be alone with Botticelli's *Venus* (he had her to himself for a full quarter of an hour), while Seasonal was stuck in the first rooms of Gothic paintings. Flat people and lots of gold. Sequences that tell a story. They immediately became a fan of the Annunciation. (*Who doesn't like to see an angel kneeling at a woman's feet?*) An ox and an ass in every nativity. They stayed in those early rooms and looked and looked, marveling at what was possible before perspective.

Seasonal much prefers the showy Roman Catholic churches of Italy to the austere Dutch Reform churches of the Netherlands. Their favorite thing about Saint Martin's Cathedral in Utrecht is the traces of the devastation wrought on the decorations by the Iconoclastic Fury of 1566, in which the Calvinists chiseled the faces off every single relief and tomb. Such focused, dedicated anger. The outside of the cathedral is glorious, the inside plain. In Italy it is the reverse. The plain outside of the churches belies their rich, complex, fantastical interiors. Naively, Seasonal thinks Italian churches are like people: pretty boring on the outside, astounding on the inside. The first time they walked into a church in Rome—a nondescript white building with no visible windows—they were speechless and moved. *For all the horrors of organized religion, and Catholicism in particular ... there is this?*

Entering the Basilica of Santa Maria Novella two hours before closing time, they are tired but hopeful.

There are a number of frescoes that inspire their interest, but it is the Tornabuoni Chapel, painted between 1485 and 1490 by Domenico Ghirlandaio and his workshop, that floors them. It is the blockbuster of the basilica and they stand, tears in their eyes, for they don't know how long, looking at the faces, the tableaus, the gestures, the fabrics. A figure with arms outstretched in perfect symmetry toward a crying child. A man in a crowd looks away from his interlocutor and straight out of the picture to them. A woman stands in profile with improbably straight posture in a gold brocade gown.

Seasonal has no desire to read art history about these paintings or to know the religious tradition from which these events emerge. They want to stand in front of them in deep ignorance, and weep.

People come and go from the chapel, some of them glance at Seasonal, who is weeping and looking upward. Their parents would be horrified that they are so easily mistaken for a pilgrim, or a local moved by the Spirit. In fact, Seasonal is crying in the presence of audacity, humor, precision, determination. Looking at these flat paintings, they fall in love with the imaginations of long-dead painters.

All these people kneeling. All this beseeching. All this acceptance. Such peacefulness. The destruction is rarely depicted. What is absent from these images is the force required to instill the Will of God, the Will of the Church, in the hearts and minds of all these peaceful, quirky people depicted holding impossibly proportioned lambs, or standing in beautifully flowing robes. But the violence is there. A trace. And the knowledge of the violence and suffering cannot be ignored when looking at these images.

And it is the violence, not the beauty or the peace, that Seasonal is seeking now.

From Florence, they travel by train to Prato, then to Parma (via Modena). At the end of the journey, Seasonal lies in bed in their hotel room in Parma, chatting in WhatsApp with László. They discuss obedience. And after they fall asleep, László types into the dark. He is confused. He is trying to find his way into submission. Seasonal knows he has to climb over the enormous wall of entitlement and egocentrism that sequesters him from the world. This wall keeps him isolated in what Eileen Myles calls "monotonous male reality." They have to help him get out, coax him out, be patient as he fumbles his way around the escape room that has been built for him by the patriarchy. As they walk down the wide stairs in the internal courtyard of the historic villa that is now a hotel, it is Sunday morning and they are looking forward to an Italian breakfast. They swell with benevolent patience and the slow realization that they will punish him today.

I stand ready.

Seeing this message in the morning, they respond:

> *i hope you mean*
> *you stand ready to*
> *learn.*

I wish I had
the opportunity to
prove myself.

In the power exchange, it is Seasonal's job not to coddle him, and so they speak more directly than they have ever dared.

> *you have had them.*

After exploring Parma, in the afternoon they make their way to the train station and begin the two-and-a-half-hour journey to Prato. As they take their seat in the carriage, they take out their phone and return to the chat with László, who is home in Amsterdam.

hello.

are you still here?

yes.

László seems to have lost his capital letters. They ask him to describe where he is. He reports that he is sitting in an armchair, clothed,

*working on a
manuscript, writing
conclusions.*

*clearly i don't have
your full attention.*

*i try to manage
my anxiety with
pretending to do
some work.*

He is outside his comfort zone. Right where they want him to be.

*can you feel my
will through the
device you are using?*

*i'm not sure i
understand the question.*

when you read
these words

when you see
my typing

do you feel my
will is present
to you?

i moved from my
mobile to my
laptop, so i can
express myself
more conveniently.

your words rest
on my lap.

:)

i need to know
if you feel my
will in this
exchange.

i am going to
reach for you
there in your
armchair, but you
have to tell me
if you feel it.

my body and
mind react

to your presence

good

He tells them the steel cock ring he is wearing is a notch tighter. He is not wearing underwear, and the fabric of his jeans causes him pain. Earlier that day, when he had said he wanted to serve them, the promise was accompanied by a beautifully framed black-and-white dick pic and the confession: *this is my raw desire to serve you.* The cock ring catching the light, his wrist at a sharp right angle to his horizontal erection, almost as precise as the posture of the woman in the fresco.

As the train moves away from Parma, László has confirmed their typed words on the screen affect him, and Seasonal's curiosity and desire is piqued. They will punish him while they ride the trains through Tuscany.

László will be punished for marking himself in secret. Seasonal thinks he likes to walk around, or sit in his armchair, seeing himself in submission. He fails to understand that when he has truly submitted to them, he will have lost himself entirely. There will be nothing for him to see, there will be no position outside himself available.

For now, on the train, they know they have to scare him and make him feel sick. And now that they have confirmed his attention is locked into the screen, they begin the scene.

The train from Parma is approaching Bologna. László has marked his chest with the pencil and sent a selfie confirming its presence.

> *the mark on your*
> *chest is mine too*

> *you made a*
> *mistake, do you*
> *know what it is?*

no please tell
me

> *i have taught*
> *you this lesson*
> *already*

> *you did not*
> *pay attention*

                                              why should i
                                              tell you again?

The train is hot and airless. But they are breathing a sweet cool air of
this new way of speaking.

                                              it would be
                                              better to punish
                                              you so you
                                              learn, surely

...

                                              you are confused?

no. i'm ashamed.

you are right, i
probably missed
something that i
should have paid
attention to.

i fear your
punishment, but
i feel i
deserve it.

*i don't care
if you think
you deserve it.*

*the important thing
is that you realize
you have made a
mistake.*

*how long would
you like to
experience the dread
of punishment?*

*i don't know what
is worse, the fear
of the unknown,
or the dread felt
over the known.*

The train rocks gently, and they are dimly aware of other passengers in the carriage. The exchange sends Seasonal deep within themself—within their body which swells with lust—while also drawing them into an interstitial flowing space that is made by the words they are exchanging with László. He describes his erection, his fear, his desire. Seasonal knows that fear is time, and so they tell him he will have to wait ten minutes before he knows his punishment. They fill the time with a lecture on how forgetful he is, and he reciprocates by explicating his shame. Then he grovels.

you have only let
me experience a
glimpse of your power,
i fear to open
that door even
more slightly.

                                            why?

i don't know
whether i can
remain standing
in front of it.

Their pride swells. The blood rushes between their legs. But László has already told them that he finds *kneeling easy*, and so they also recognize the submissive hyperbole.

                                  do you like
                               that feeling? or
                           does it overwhelm
                                   you?

yes. i like it.
yes. it overwhelms
me.

They know what he means. When they allow themself to feel it, their desire to take him to the point of annihilation drowns their senses. The train disappears and they are focused solely on domination through the tiny screen, through the keyboard, through the data connection.

there is one minute left of your ten minutes.

do you still feel like you deserve punishment?

i know.

i do.

what is your safe word?

counting back from ten to one

oh jesus

The black heart emoji appears.

Sitting on the train and scaring László as he sits in his apartment in Amsterdam feels like sex. Seasonal is surprised to experience the release of hormones they associate with physical encounters.

my heart is in
my throat there
is a wet stain
under me i
feel adrenalin
pushing me to
fight or flight

> *go to your*
> *kitchen and make*
> *a saline solution.*
> *do you know*
> *how to do that?*

There is a pause. Seasonal is dimly aware of the riot of color that is the landscape passing outside the train window.

i so far made
3 fl. oz. of
solution stronger
than seawater

> *you need three*
> *cups of it*

Another pause. Seasonal's pelvis softens with desire.

i have 3 cups
of saline solution
as you asked

here is what you
are going to do:
drink two of
the cups of saline
handwrite a
list of things you
know bring me
pleasure
handwrite a
list of what you
know i am trying
to achieve in
our collaboration
send me
a photograph of
each list.

Forty minutes later, Seasonal paces back and forth on a city block behind the Florence train station. A light rain falls. They are talking with László, the two of them trying to understand what has just happened between them.

It is nice to hear you laugh in astonishment, he says over the crackling data connection.

Hours later, after eating gelati and walking around the medieval center of Prato with her friend, Seasonal lies in the dark in the guest bedroom in the three-bedroom apartment. Through the closed door they can hear the couple making plans for tomorrow, the low mumble of domestic logistics.

A message arrives.

Thank you for
today.

For you attention.
Care. Discipline.

I would like to
somehow give you
back the gift you
gave me today
as physical pleasure
as a wet stain
a scent on your
face a touch
on your skin

They pull the phone closer.

may i ask
where are you?

                                                    i am lying in
                                                         bed.

                                                    in the dark.

are you comfortable
with reading my
words?

                                                              yes.

i would like to
make love to you
with my words
you don't have to
type just stay with
me with your eyes
i need your hands
elsewhere on your
breasts i don't
know if you can
inflict pain on
yourself or you
would need my
hand for that
but i want you
to pinch your right
nipple the way you
pinched mine

i want you to
feel the pain
you gave me
today
i want you to
know that it
made me wet
and hard.
i want you to
know that pure
anticipation pushed
me to the edge
of orgasm and
i wanted to
bury my head to
the sweet, heavy
scent of your lap
to cover my shame
if you were here,
i would have
begged you not
to do what you
did to me
i want you to
touch yourself,
and touch your
sex hard with
the same power
you subjected me
with the same pride

with the same fullness
with the same
existential certainty

Seasonal's orgasm is sharp and wide. An exhilarating tearing at their center that begins in the contact point between their hand and their clitoris and ends somewhere beyond the edges of the known universe.

As they fall asleep, they wonder: *Is it László or the phone that is fucking me?*

An Unexpected Exchange

Two days later, Seasonal is walking through Schiphol Plaza toward the train platform. They dodge tourists wearing large winter coats and pulling equally large suitcases toward the train to Amsterdam. On the platform, they take out their phone to listen to music, and a message arrives from László.

I know how power
and dominance is
displayed by/
through the male
body

But I never had
the chance to
experience the same
by/through
the female body

Apart from the
superficial and
artificial roles in
femdom kink.

I would be immensely
grateful if you could
show me this
substance I currently
have no way to
express

Properly, or at all

This is their aim, and they write back, telling him just this. But they also see László's inability to imagine that the form of female power is structural, cultural, and they tell him that too. The culture does not trade in genuine female power. The train to Utrecht arrives and they ponder this larger question; by the time they have found a seat, László has responded.

I long for a
feeling which I
know exists but
I have no firsthand
experience of.

May I share my
naked sexuality with
you now?

                                                            yes.

In the past I
have been pegged
by a woman.
There wasn't, however,
a power component,
though I wish it
had.

                                                            ...
                                            there is a very
                                    significant overlap
                                            in our desires
                                                        here.

The black heart emoji appears.

I beg for a
more detailed
explanation.

Seasonal needs to buy some time. They are not sure if they should tell him about the Parisian, about being called *boy*, about the fact that they might be very good at what the modern world is calling *pegging* but which they like to think of with its biblical term: *sodomy.*

i want to hear
you say please.

They instruct him to record a voice message asking for the explanation. László dutifully does so, and the message arrives swiftly. In his voice they hear the confidence that he will get an answer when he asks them to *share with me your desires, Seasonal, please.* The sound they hear is deeply irritating. It is the voice of someone who is not used to asking more than once.

that sounds like
curiosity not begging

Twenty minutes later, as the train pulls in to Utrecht, another voice file arrives:

You are right. The last time it was the curiosity that was speaking, now I am literally on my knees. Not because I'm begging, but more out of respect for what you are going to say, and out of respect for the trust you place in me by sharing your deepest and worst desires. And I would like to tell you how much I appreciate if you do that. So please, share your desires with me, Seasonal.

Through their headphones, they hear the humility. They are fascinated that he must point out he is not begging. At least he tried.

To reward his effort, Seasonal responds with an edited version of the text they had written on the plane to Florence. The text had spilled out of them in a furtive, almost blind kind of wishing which flushed them with shame as it poured through their fingers onto the screen:

Sitting on the plane to Florence I think about László's asshole. I want to fuck him, and I want him to beg me to do it. I want to feel the female end of the double dildo the Parisian gave me shift with the pressure as the male end fills László, while I possess him with it, while I take him beyond his edges through his body and queer him.

László's response is immediate.

I beg you now,
as I will beg you
on my knees when
we next meet, to
find me worthy
of fucking me.

Seasonal is dizzy. They are overcome with a breathless sense of urgency. In two weeks they leave for Australia—their first trip home since emigrating. Can this busy husband and father find time to be fucked before Seasonal has to leave for six weeks? They try to coolly propose a meeting, but they are liquifying at the prospect of what has just emerged as a very real possibility.

The negotiations are efficient and successful. With relief, Seasonal asks:

do you need my
address?

I remember.

The path.

Nine days later, Seasonal takes an afternoon walk in the dying light. It is the day before László's visit. With the leaves gone from the trees, everything seems a lot closer. Exposed. Spaces that seemed protected and expansive in the summer now appear small and empty.

Seasonal walks knowing their power lies in what they do not say. They have to use this silence to get to where they need to go. As they walk in the newly bare space of the nature reserve, the grass brown, the sky colorless, they walk with the knowledge that they must keep their motivation hidden, their pleasure partly obscured, in order not to lose the opportunity to keep using him and his curiosity.

Walking swiftly in parallel to a small canal, they ask themself: *How much compassion do men deserve? And can we be compassionate toward them without denying ourselves?*

The following afternoon it is cold and dry. László arrives and Seasonal offers him tea. The two sit opposite each other at Seasonal's small dining room table, and László observes that the reality that they are strangers to each other plays a role in what they are doing. He would like to preserve it, somehow.

This is why I did not want your address, he tells them. *I have to remember my way back to this place, this woman. It is a problem of memory. If I have your address, it is a Google Maps problem.*

Seasonal smiles and avoids speculating on why he can only be this honest about his desires with a stranger. They invite him upstairs. They take his face in their hands and kiss him softly. Then each quickly undresses. László lies naked on their white sheets, his entire body a hungry question. Seasonal takes the double dildo and harness out of the small cupboard that sits beside their bed. He looks at the bulbous female end.

Can you take it? He is cautious.

Yes, Seasonal responds happily.

László takes the matte silicone object from their hand and puts the entire female end in his mouth. It emerges shiny, bright with his spit, a conspiratorial and happy light shines in his eyes. Seasonal is already liquid, becomes more so watching this pragmatic gesture. He hands the object to them and they slip it into place, emitting a long and low sigh. They grip it with the complex network of muscles that knit their pelvis. They are full but not satisfied. It makes them hungrier. The two of them work efficiently together to fit the harness around the prosthesis and Seasonal's hips and ass. When it is secure, Seasonal looms above him on their knees, facing him with their erection.

You have a beautiful dick. It suits you. László is beaming. Seasonal smiles, having no sense of what will come next but feeling confidently curious.

Why have you bought a dick? He asks, bristling with admiration and excitement. Seasonal stumbles through an answer about the gift of penetration. They tell László they want to feel that they are giving. They can barely speak as the female end teases their desire, and László lies before them, open, willing, curious.

As they kneel over him with their dick pointing toward him, their left hand rubbing the shaft slowly with lubricant, they avoid his question about whether or not they have fucked anyone with their dick before. They are struck by the external, undeniable symbol of László's effect on them. *A wet cunt is a secret* ... Seasonal dimly realizes ... *this* ... *is* ... *not* ...

They lean forward, intuitively adjusting their pelvis between László's spread legs. As they gently enter him he undergoes an instant transformation. He is an entirely different beauty in this moment. Moving below them, moving on them, allowing them further inside him. Welcoming them into an unexpected exchange.

Afterward, László goes home and Seasonal starts packing. Soon they will return to Australia. They do not know what to think about this imminent return to a land that burns after a small number of years in the land the freezes. They have a blunt intuition that this distinction is important, it could tell them something, but they do not know what it could be.

The Old Violence

Two days later Seasonal leaves behind the depressing winter darkness and boards a plane. They take with them the sound of László's happy voice saying *fantastic* and the look of sheer gratitude he gave them after they had sodomized him many times. They were pleased that this exchange of positions had produced a surprising symmetry between them: their greed to possess him was matched by his greediness to feel them inside him. But as they drag their suitcase across Schiphol Plaza, they are relieved to be leaving. They need some respite from all the newness and all the breaking. They are flying back to what they know, and while there is some trepidation about their return, they take comfort in anticipating the relief from the experience of being a foreigner.

Seasonal is returning to the land where they had stalkers. It is easy to be a stalker in a small country town in rural Australia. Especially if you own a car. Their first stalker was slightly older than them: he had his driver's license and a car. Seasonal was fifteen and still condemned to walk everywhere or ask their parents to drive them places. Her first stalker's name was Glenn. He was too thin, too short, and very quiet. His lank brown hair sat limp on his shoulders. He smoked and worked at the local bottle shop, and so he had more money than most of the people Seasonal knew. She guessed this is why he always had petrol in his car. Glenn would drive slowly past Seasonal's house every day after school. His small red hatchback, always covered in light dust from the country roads, would appear: at parties, in the main street of the next town up the highway where Seasonal went to meet friends, near the high school. Seasonal came to associate its slow crawl along the street with a vague ominous feeling of being held responsible for her vitality. Glenn would sometimes leave things at the front door of her house: chocolates, flowers, brief notes of supplication in his straggly handwriting. Seasonal would throw these things away, unopened.

On Valentine's Day—the day stalkers feel most like martyrs—Glenn left a large, pristine white teddy bear on the doorstep, holding a red rose. Seasonal's mother found it and brought it inside. She thought it was lovely. *I want to cut it into pieces*, Seasonal said in her sullen teenager voice. *He is a creep. He follows me everywhere.* The mother thought the daughter should be more grateful for the attention, that the bear deserved to be cherished. She took the white bear and kept it. For years it sat in Seasonal's mother's bedroom, on the small wall-mounted bookshelf that her older brother had made in woodworking class. Two decades later, when Seasonal left Australia for the Netherlands, the bear moved too. It now sits in a spare bedroom of the family home in that same town in rural Australia, on the bespoke bookshelves Seasonal had made to celebrate getting tenure at a university in Melbourne but which they could not ship across the world. The bookshelves hold their mother's small library of contemporary fiction, sentimental items, toys for the grandchildren to play with when they visit. These things sit alongside the bear she would not let her daughter destroy.

It is early morning. Seasonal's jet lag is almost gone; they are no longer between worlds, they have almost arrived. They are walking in the dawn light along the beach. They are chatting with László.

And to be frank,
there is nothing I
desire more than
being overpowered, to
lose, to the point
of my total annihilation,
capitulation, and submission.

Seasonal is south of Sydney, in a small coastal town that sits on a slither of land below a towering escarpment. They are visiting Y. In the first week of their visit, Y leads Seasonal on a long bush walk up the escarpment through burnt, low-growing scrub. She walks in bare feet on the rocky path, but Seasonal needs shoes. Y scales the path like a mountain goat—she has walked this cliff a lot. A few years ago, she would walk for hours up here. She would walk alone on the cliff face, in the thick scrub of the coastal bush, walking off and walking into her frustration and pain. Today Y is walking pain again, but this time she is not walking it alone. Seasonal's eyes are adjusting to Australia; the light, the brilliant big sky, the warm orange of the sandstone rocks. The hot, sweet smell of the gums further off. This bushland burns often, and a fire went through here last year. The regrowth on the banksias is fluorescent and jubilant. Seasonal keeps being distracted by the dark chambers of the burnt banksia cones that lie on the ground: transformed into charcoal by the flames, holding their form, they are stark against the grey granite and white sand that cover the top of the escarpment. Seasonal looks down the coastline toward the small town where Y lives with her daughter and her mother. They look out at the expanse of the South Pacific Ocean. They look back into the thick bush across the top of the cliff face. All this space. Unimaginable space. They talk their pain about H. Y talks her pain about her boyfriend. Neither of them really know what to do with their feelings, except to feel them and to walk.

After the walk, Seasonal and Y sit together in the car at the central beach in the small coastal town, watching the surfers head out for the evening swell.

When we were in bed on Saturday morning, Y tells them as she takes a long drag on the cigarette they are sharing, *he was holding my wrist and moving me around to cuddle me in a different way. It felt nice, it felt good, and then it didn't. I said, "Let go of my wrist." He didn't let go. He said, "I am going to dominate you." I said, "Let go of my wrist." And he did.* She pauses and watches the pair of cockatoos stripping the bark from a nearby tree. *All the shit he gave me about vanilla sex for the last three years, but he just had a list in his head of things he wanted done. He was not having sex with me.* Y's face is blank with anger. The birds continue stripping the tree, and Seasonal holds their friend in their gaze.

Later that night, after everyone else is in bed, Seasonal researches Hungarian politics. The enormous gap in their knowledge about where László is from is beginning to feel like a problem. While there are some Hungarians in Australia, there was not a discernible wave of arrivals from that part of Europe over Australia's long and schizophrenic history of using immigration as a core strategy for dispossessing First Nations people of their land. Seasonal

has a working knowledge of the economic and political crises that drove people into exile from China, Italy, Greece, Macedonia, Lebanon, Germany, Vietnam, Cambodia, the former Yugoslavia, the Sudan, Iran, Iraq, India, and Pakistan. Seasonal has an incomplete mental sketch of ethnic majorities and minorities, of economic crises, colonial legacies and decolonial struggles, which countries have had despotic governments or armies that had a tendency to overturn elections, and which were unsafe for women, homosexuals, and the working poor. In some cases, more than one generation of people had come to Australia to find a way out of circumstances that were some version of unbearable, and in those cases, such as Italy and Greece, Australia and parts of Europe felt quite intimately connected. Seasonal had a sense of what communism had done to Asia, but the Soviet period and what it really meant for people in Eastern Europe was a black hole in Seasonal's knowledge. They had caught a glimpse of what they did not know when they had dated a fellow student at university whose father had had his jaw broken for being a member of Solidarność. Seasonal's boyfriend was awkwardly, ambivalently Polish, like many of the children of migrants Seasonal knew, but his father was joyously Polish. Seasonal stayed longer in the relationship than she really wanted to because she found his father so lovely, open, informative, weird. She relished the conversations they would have over breakfast, or while her boyfriend and his younger sister played *Tomb Raider* on rainy Sunday afternoons.

Seasonal lies in bed and scrolls, learning that Hungary's history is marked by empires. Having been raised in the remnants of the British Empire, Seasonal thinks of empires as a particular formation of gender, language, race, and power. Not terribly interested in a history lesson, Seasonal starts their research with the present—the parliamentary elections held earlier this year, in which Viktor Orbán had increased his majority. The political opposition is in disarray, unable to unify against Orbán's version of what Hungary could be. Orbán's government recently removed gender studies from the list of government-approved master's programs and is pushing family-friendly economic measures which are underpinned by fears of a demographic catastrophe. Sexual intimacy and raising children in Orbán's Hungary are things one does in service of the government's vision of society. A few more searches lead to Seasonal reading about the worsening situation of independent media, and the rising anti-immigration rhetoric. All this is familiar to Seasonal, who has been watching the rise of nationalist-patriarchal thinking for most of their adult life. *But what is Hungarian about all this?* Seasonal asks. They believe that understanding this will help them understand László's relationship to gender and power and desire. A few more Google searches and Seasonal finds some details about Orbán's story of Hungary in an unverified translation of Orbán's speech to Parliament at the beginning of his fourth mandate, in May 2018.

If we want to decide what Hungarians can aspire to in the world, we must not ignore our size. Over the past 1,100 years this has continually changed, but we have never been among the world's most populous nations. The situation today is that Hungarians account for 0.2 percent of the total world population. From this it clearly follows that the survival of Hungarians as a nation is not automatic. Hungarian policy ... should be predicated on the possibility that we could disappear, we could be dispersed, we could become extinct, and the world could go on without that species of Homo sapiens known as the Hungarians ... We are a unique species. We have a language that is unique to us. There is a world which we alone see and which we alone render through the prism of

Hungarian language and culture. Without us human civilization would certainly be deprived of a language, a view, and a characterization of the world. This must sustain the firm resolve of the government of the day. In the outside world the government should present itself and represent Hungary in the knowledge that we have achieved a great deal, and that we have contributed to the sum total of human achievement in science, culture, sport, and the arts. We must have the confidence and dignity of a country which knows that the Hungarians have given more to the world than they have taken from it. Our achievements give us the right to continue our history.

Seasonal quickly notices that Orbán's tale of Hungary centers on the idea that to be Hungarian is to be small, to be a minority. This is the power source for his rhetoric. More reading shows them that this is not a story Orbán invented, it is a very old story about Hungary that the Hungarians tell. The ontology of Hungary becomes clear: no one can become Hungarian, it is a birthright. Seasonal realizes this is an important point of difference with the conservatism they had escaped: for Australian conservatives, anyone can become an Australian, as long as they are prepared to cast off all elements of themselves that are incompatible with the conservative definition of national character and behavior. But Hungarians are born, and they are born into a responsibility to be Hungarian. And to be Hungarian, for Orbán, is to speak a language no one else speaks, and to adhere to Christian values. Seasonal feels the rush of insight: it is an orderly and compelling narrative to weave in order to be able to declare liberal democracy a failed project in Europe. The Hungarians are exquisitely suspended by Orbán's logic, trapped by their very identity. You are Hungarian, you are vulnerable, you must be my version of Hungarian if you are to survive. Like many patriarchs, Orbán tells a story of circumstantial impotence to justify violence and domination. That is familiar enough to Seasonal from their father's behavior.

But what does this help them understand about László's desire to be overpowered, to lose, to capitulate? They are fairly confident he is not a closet fascist, waiting for his moment to turn the tables and use his disempowerment as a justification for violence. So why does he want it? And why do they want to give him this opportunity to encounter annihilation? Perhaps all László is looking for are brief moments of respite from the existential struggle of trying to keep alive a minority culture and language with his partner and child and Hungarian friends. Maybe he just wants a break from the anxiety of existence. Seasonal realizes they know nothing, really, about the wounds the Soviet Empire created, nor the older wounds it covered over or reinfected. The Europeans that Seasonal encountered in Australia and through Australian culture are, by and large, the ones who walked away from the task of trying to come to grips with European history, the way Seasonal is trying to walk away from their family history. The Europeans in Europe are the ones who wrestle.

Seasonal slips out the back door and walks down the steep hill toward the beach, their head spinning. They walk along the beach in the dark, listening to the waves of the Pacific Ocean, and then crawl into bed around 2:00 a.m. They wonder what they have gotten themself into. In moving to Europe, they are a product of the new world in the Old World, a product of racist-patriarchal violence trying to find their way out of a story written into their desire.

The next day they return to the task at hand. They are focused on helping Y break up with the asshole she has inadvertently fallen in love with. The first time Seasonal met this asshole boyfriend, almost three years ago, the hair on the back of their neck stood up. He has spent three years *undermining and love-bombing* Y. Seasonal agrees with Y's mother—who has survived Y's violent alcoholic father by thirty years and counting—that the boyfriend is bad news. They are both afraid of what he might be capable of, and speak about it in low tones hidden under the sound of the electric kettle coming to a boil in the mornings while Y is fixing her daughter breakfast.

Seasonal is helping Y put into place the infrastructure she needs to break free of him. She is scared; she cannot see her way out and feels trapped and anxious. When they see her flighty energy they know the relationship has been abusive. That, and *the fucking outrageous things he has been saying and doing for three years*, tell them both that Y has to get out.

They sit together in Y's art studio—a mezzanine space in a large corrugated-iron shed that becomes unbearably hot after 10:00 a.m.—and draw a flow chart of the abusive dynamic while Y's daughter listens to music on her pink headphones and gives two Monster High dolls a makeover using scissors and markers. Seasonal tells Y the truth about the abusive mindset: the pleasure in denial, the flood of gratification that comes from belittling another and thinking you know everything. The megalomaniacal belief that *if everyone just did what I said, what they were told, then there would be no problems.* The actual brain-altering chemicals that are released when you sense the fear you instill in the other. They give Y the language beyond rationality for this, as she keeps asking *How can he treat someone this way?* How? Circuits of gratification, impulse, the sense of power that comes from pretending that you are listening to someone speak because you know the other wants to be listened to, all the while your muscles are tingling with the knowledge that what they say is irrelevant. Omnipotence.

Y has never tangled with a man like this before. Seasonal was raised by one. They know how they work.

Y writes phrases on index cards and puts them near her door, so she knows what to say if he arrives unannounced. They talk about whom she can call when she is lonely and list all the parts of her life—her daughter, her art practice, her friendships—that she can focus on when she is missing him or feeling afraid.

That evening, Seasonal records the sound of the summer thunderstorm as it rolls out over the high cliffs toward the ocean. The sharp crack of the thunder, the blanketing sound of the downpour. They cannot record the smell that is released by rain: the bright fragrance of hot asphalt becoming wet, the scent of wood and eucalyptus from the trees that fills the air. The stored heat in the ground meeting the coolness of the rain.

The next day, Seasonal sits on the floor of Y's living room, reiterating the importance of Y acknowledging that being an asshole brings the asshole boyfriend actual pleasure. They are speaking out of their confidence, but then they find themself saying something they do not expect: *I know this. Because I have experienced this pleasure. When I deny, when I outsmart, when I corner László, I get high from it. Nothing else is like the high I get from it, and I can become quite fixated on pursuing it.*

Seasonal falls silent. They don't know where to look. They do not say they want to annihilate László. That they want to destroy him. That the thought of him losing himself through the pain, restrictions, anxiety, and the pleasure they might be able to bring him thrills them. That the fear of obliteration that Y is trying to outmaneuver is the fear they are trying to create.

The two friends look at each other across the tan carpet, the small blue ceramic teapot, the empty teacups, the remaining Mint Slice cookie alone on the plate, beading water as it moves to room temperature. Y does not judge them. Seasonal tries to feel no shame. They distract themselves with a game of Cat Bingo with Y's daughter, laughing as the young girl renames the cat breeds after actors and characters from the new *Star Wars* films Seasonal has not seen because they have no children.

A few days later, Seasonal says goodbye and rides the train up the coast to fly to Melbourne. Their mind is awash with images of László's boyish smile, László handling rope, László's beautiful proud stance and their pulsing drive to subdue and own him. Their body fires with the thin, high energy of lust.

But they are also deeply cautious and chided by this brush with the regularity of gendered violence, of men's belief in their inherent dominance over the body they see as female, with the brutality of having to talk frankly with a seventy-nine-year-old survivor of a violent marriage about whether or not she thinks her daughter's boyfriend will physically harm the three generations of women that live in the house. As the train turns away from the ocean toward the endless suburbs of Sydney, they feel the familiar weight in their body that they came to understand in their twenties as shame and sadness. This weight registers the deep reality that no one was able to help their mother break the spell of abuse their father wove into their marriage. In a few hours Seasonal will be sleeping in their childhood home, which has known all kinds of violence, which rests on such unhappy and unequal foundations. They look at suburbia unfurling outside the window and struggle with their similarity to the abuser and the strange, compelling intensities of finding consensual ways to open the circuits of gratification they have hopefully helped Y escape.

Survival is a question of life force, Orbán told his colleagues in the Hungarian Parliament. Seasonal can't disagree.

Seasonal only lasts two days in the town where they grew up before they need a respite visit to Melbourne. They sit in Q's backyard in the baking northern suburbs, eating Thai salad. They tell Q about their fear of being like the abuser, and when they mention that their mother told them, just yesterday, while assembling a salad, how much they are like their father, and how they struggle with this near-constant reminder from everyone in the family that they resemble him, Q says quickly and forcefully:

But you know you are not like him, right?

They want to believe him.

Seasonal watches Q roll a cigarette. László wants them to bring their desires to him, but they have spent hours and hours walking, washing dishes, cooking meals, hanging laundry, walking to classes, riding their bicycle, sitting in meetings held in Dutch, buying vegetables, on airplanes, in elevators, wondering: *How do you tell someone you want to destroy them?*

On December 30, Y drives to Melbourne with her daughter and the three of them ring in the new year together, maintaining Y's struggle to free herself from the abusive dynamic. She sees that the relationship was abusive, and now comes the shame. *How? Why?* The things that were said. The things that were done. Y shares with Seasonal a phenomenal email exchange between the two of them that signals the endgame has begun. Y's parting line is:

You love as deeply as you loathe.

Y is staying with Seasonal in a housesit, deep in the Melbourne suburb of Brunswick. The house is a 1990s townhouse that is modeled on the turn-of-the-century terrace houses that cluster in Melbourne's inner-city suburbs. Once working class, these dingy, badly ventilated houses have narrow faces and run long down the block. The originals, and these knockoffs, are now highly sought after because of gentrification. This 1990s version is uglier than the originals; the developer would not spend the money on the brickwork and tuck-pointing that makes a terrace house mildly architectural. The bricks are rendered and painted apricot, and the building does not have the heavy wooden sash windows of its template. Instead it has aluminum awning windows that only open from the bottom, operated with a tiny wheeled mechanism. It is not possible to get a breeze going in this house, and the bedrooms remain stifling. Across the street are the slightly less ugly freestanding houses known as California bungalows, with sash windows and wider street frontage. These are the larger houses that stretch for dozens of square kilometers across Melbourne's suburbs, and which—in their unrenovated form—were the staple of the student housing Seasonal lived in for the six years it took them to get their undergraduate degree.

As they meander through Melbourne together, seeking respite in the air-conditioned art galleries and cafés, Y identifies the contours of the asshole boyfriend's misogyny. Seasonal is in awe of their friend's clarity and power to name what she has lived.

Y barely survived her encounter with abusive masculinity in a condensed and pure form. She feels that he was trying to destroy her. They walk in the blistering city and talk constantly about his actions. When the two of them take a break from talking, Seasonal's mind turns to their desire for László's destruction. They want to do what the abusive man Y has had to flee was trying to do. They want to annihilate László's will and subjectivity and install themself in him. They want to absolutely control his emotional register—to have and use the power to bring him ecstasy and pain, humiliation and desperation, denial and rejection. They want him to live in fear of them. They want him to feel joy because they (and only they) can give it to him, and they want him to feel crushing abyssal sadness when he cannot be proximate to them, his sole source of joy and pleasure. They want him entirely to themself, to allow him connections to the outside world only so that he can know the shallowness, the paucity of those connections in comparison to his connection to them. They want to preoccupy that sharp mind and strong bullshit filter and be the object of its fixation.

They feel so ashamed to think these things, to give them form in their consciousness, that they can only do so sitting alone in the dark when Y and her daughter have gone to sleep.

It seems impossible to tell László that they want to ruin his life and own him. Of course, they do not really want this—they like and respect him, and have consented to their relationship knowing that he is committed to his partner and child—and yet within the game, whose limits they do not fully know or feel, they are surprised by the clarity and intensity of the desire. They are beginning to realize that fear and physical pain are the mechanisms of annihilation, that through the giving of physical pain, and thus creating the fear of pain, they instill themself in László in a way that approximates the total mastery and will to master that they desire, and which they can never achieve. Unlike Y, who was sparring with a ruthless dom unwittingly and without giving consent, László has explicitly invited them to seek pleasure in his annihilation. When he agreed to be punished while they rode the trains in Italy, he consented to fear, he submitted to their will, and he committed himself to do whatever it was they asked him to do. The fear he felt when they asked his safe word, his desire to flee from the scene of submission in South Korea when he was jetlagged were fleeting but tangible and inexplicable moments when they had him.

They feel a growing determination to learn how to extend those brief moments into longer scenes. To extend for him the suspension of his will, which he desires and fears, and prolong their moments of ownership. They see now the role that giving real pain plays in this: their grip on his testicles, their teeth in the taut flesh of his chest, the sting of the palm of their hand on his skin. They see it because they watch Y struggle to free herself from a man who genuinely frightened her, who intimidated her, a man who demanded her submission and pursued it through force, manipulation, and intimidation. They see now why their mother can never make a decision for herself, why she was unable to leave their father. The moment of submission can become extended, can become routine, can become a kind of safety despite the degradation and pain it entails.

They are horrified and intrigued by these connections. They peer at the clots, tangles, and knots that are the ossified destructive power relation of gendered violence. They stare at the scene of their family life, of their childhood. They wonder whether these small games they play with László are meaningless in the face of it, whether those clots, tangles, and knots can be pried out of their usual configuration using consent, physical attraction, negotiation, Foucault and made into something else using the shared power of sexuality, intellect, ethics.

As they think these things walking the baking streets of a Melbourne summer, Seasonal is unnerved by the grandiosity of their desire. They are afraid. But the newly found power of their combined intelligence and sexuality makes them, again, eerily and profoundly confident.

When Seasonal's head was still shaved, she lived in a dilapidated California bungalow a few kilometers from the housesit. While studying literature and philosophy at university, Seasonal did theatre as an extracurricular activity. Theatre gave her a way to use her vitality for her own pleasure. She did theatre with some older students, and as summer approached the group began discussing forming a theatre troupe to stage a performance for an upcoming Fringe Festival. Two of the boys in the group were insistent that Jason be included in the group. Jason mainly did tech for the student theatre productions, but he would have liked to act, to write, perhaps to direct. Jason was tall, big-boned, and blonde. He had a nervous energy and bad skin. He talked over people, mostly female people, and he sometimes stood too close. When he stood too close, Seasonal could smell his breath. She guessed that Jason had never kissed anyone, because he would not let his breath smell that way if he had. None of the women in the fledging theatre group wanted Jason to be involved in the performance. Improvising theatre involved trust, an openness to touch and physical intimacy, a willingness to play and be played with. None of the women wanted to do that with Jason. Their intuition spoke loud. Seasonal spoke quietly to the other women in the group about her desire never to be left alone with Jason. The other women agreed. When the women said in a group meeting that they did not want Jason to be a part of the performance, that they were not comfortable with it, the men agreed the performance could not go ahead without him, and so the group disbanded.

Six months later Jason was convicted of rape. None of the men from the group acknowledged what the women had said.

The surface of Seasonal's skin remembers him. Their skin and somewhere deep in their gut, in their bowel, low, in middle of their body.

Seasonal has never been that interested in New Year's Eve. By 9:30 p.m. Y is asleep on the hardwood floor in the fake terrace house. By 10:00 p.m., Seasonal agrees with Y's daughter when she suggests that it is time that she and her mother went to bed. They accompany the two upstairs and go and lie on their bed in the front room. These are the final hours of 2018, and the heat in the room is stifling. Seasonal allows themself the indulgence of some reflection. They will not take the problems with H into the new year. Those problems can no longer be a motivation for any action: that means they must quit smoking, as they started smoking to cope with the distressing conversations they were having about their sex life.

Their phone pings; the Parisian appears.

bonsoir

> *hello. i am in*
> *australia, wondering*
> *if you have found anyone to fuck you*
> *with that beautiful*
> *cock yet.*

Not yet ;)

> *i remain hopeful :)*
> *now i have*
> *experience :)*

Hihi

;)
nice that you
are still giggling

So have you
tried it?

yes i fucked
a very nice boy
with it before
i left for
australia but he
didn't call me
boy ;)

Hihi

haha

Thinking about you
fucking your guy
with your powerful
black cock

Seasonal has always wondered about the significance of the color of the cock for the Parisian. He always mentions its color. *A design thing?* They never read the phrase *black cock* without thinking about the history of the hypersexualization of Black bodies, the demonization of Black male sexuality, the Black cock as threat and forbidden desire. One more way that sex and power have become ossified in a specifically violent configuration. They hope when they meet him and he asks them for it in person, they can discern the significance of the color and the nature of the request.

oh, you like that idea? me fucking him and not you?

He was the lucky one But I would have been pleased to take his place

i am still hoping you will :)

Mmm

he doesn't know how to beg

It is true.

OMG

and you are so good at it you always ask

so nicely
so polite and
slutty :)
so eager :)

You got me :-)

It is the last hour of 2018, the morning of New Year's Eve in Paris.

Mmm
The boy is dirty

As the fireworks go off at midnight, the Parisian sends pics of his body, offering himself to them. Seasonal tells him to *feel the bite of the zipper* on his hand as he reaches into their black jeans to free their cock. Because the Parisian has no interest in orgasms—he likes to edge—he switches out of the scene to, they expect, avoid coming.

What are you doing?

Seasonal's second stalker was introduced to her in her final year of high school by a friend from a larger town, closer to the city where everyone had to go to buy their speed in little plastic bags. He was her ex-boyfriend. Whatshisname was too thin, with long reddish hair down his back. At a boozy party at her friend's house in the larger town, Seasonal awoke early in the grey predawn morning amongst the dozen or so sleeping teenaged bodies on the floor. Whatshisname was gently stroking her hair and staring at her face. When Seasonal asked him sharply what he was doing he replied with the cliché that no woman ever wants to hear: *You are beautiful when you sleep.*

His ex-girlfriend was the courier that Valentine's Day. She came to school with roses and a teddy bear to give Seasonal, who threw both in the bin, along with the handwritten card, which she did not bother to read. She was angry at the ex-girlfriend for acting as the mule, but she had no words for it so listened to Tool on her discman and smoked on the football field.

Their visit to Australia is ending. Seasonal spends the days enjoying mangos, the heat, the way their accent has broadened in the weeks they've been here. Over the time they've spent in Melbourne a strange desire has formed: Seasonal wants to put something in László's shoes that will press into the bottom of his feet, not pierce the flesh but press firmly and make a regular walking gait impossible.

On the final day in Melbourne, Seasonal borrows Q's car and drives to Fitzroy—to visit Brunswick Street, where they spent many happy days and nights as a student. They enter an interior design shop that has amongst its many recycled and bespoke items handmade blacksmithed objects—hooks, rails, door knobs. Their eye is caught by a little bag of handmade nails. They almost buy them, but are too shy. They will regret this shyness every day for months, but it will spark a wonderful and long-lasting conversation with László about nails. Next they visit the BDSM store they used to stand in in their twenties and not know why they were there. Now, Seasonal shops with purpose. After selecting a pair of leather wrist cuffs and small padlocks for László, the sales assistant asks them if they are looking for anything else specific.

I am looking for something to put in shoes. Something that will hurt him when he walks.

The assistant says they have nothing to put in shoes.

I am thinking nails, they say.

You are mean, the assistant says admiringly.

A blonde woman in a floral sundress browsing nearby pipes up:

I'd go with Legos.

They look at the shop assistant. They lock eyes. Impressed.

Oh, so painful, the assistant says, a hint of longing in her voice, as she rings up the cuffs and the two small locks.

Legos are good for pain but not the right aesthetic, they think walking back to the car, which they parked on a shady side street. Reaching the car, they take the small enamel pin shaped like the arrow of a computer cursor from their black T-shirt and put it in their left shoe. They stand and it pushes into the ball of their foot with a pleasing sharpness. But when they take a step it slips under their high arch and is useless.

Their final stop on this day trip to Fitzroy is the piercing studio. Seasonal has decided to repierce the hole in their left earlobe that their friend Shane had pierced with a heated needle when they were fifteen years old. Shane was tiny, dreadlocked, and lived in low-income housing without parents. Seasonal used to drink with Shane and his beautiful boyfriend. She felt kinship with these two boys because they were the weird arty kids in the small town. Seasonal liked to drink vodka until she lost consciousness. Seasonal knew that the two boys would keep her safe.

Like Shane, the apprentice in the piercing studio has pristine skin and the open, symmetrical face of an angel. He explains he will see if the hole is still open before piercing again. The titanium rod goes through with little pain, despite there having been no jewelry there for over a decade.

There is no wound, he says.

That evening they sleep in their childhood bedroom, their bags packed for the early flight to the Netherlands. Their phone pings, and the Parisian is seeking some morning contact.

You should kneel
Rubbing your big cock
And licking mine

Like a sexy boy
discovering his first
cock
Don't be shy you
sexy gay, take it in
your mouth
Taste it

The Parisian has switched them. Seasonal holds their black cock in their hand, they are begging to suck his.

                                                    i have never
                                                    sucked a cock
                                                    before

Mmm

                                                    but having you
                                                    in my mouth
                                                    and holding my
                                                    hard cock is
                                                    beautiful

A slut is born

                                                    haha :)

:)

may i cum like
this? with your
cock in my
mouth,
please?

Yes
You are such a
sweet and shy boy

They are relieved. They were not sure he would let them.

Salope
Mmm

They use Google Translate while masturbating in the room where they learned to masturbate. Afterward, they read some Foucault on their computer and furtively highlight passages from "Friendship as a Way of Life."

As far back as I remember, to want guys [garçons] was to want relations with guys. … Not necessarily in the form of a couple but as a matter of existence: how is it possible for men to be together? To live together, to share their time, their meals, their room, their leisure, their grief, their knowledge, their confidences? What is it to be "naked" among men, outside of institutional relations, family, profession, and obligatory camaraderie? It's a desire, an uneasiness, a desire-in-uneasiness that exists among a lot of people.

On the flight from Singapore to Amsterdam, Seasonal is thinking about László, about the Sound Engineer, about H. About annihilation and capitulation, vulnerability, desire that tips over into something more urgent ... need? Drives. They are thinking about violence, about force and momentum, intensity. They briefly contemplate making themself orgasm in the business-class toilet to the thought of László on all fours, saying *no* instead of *yes*. Perhaps it is his *no* they need to seek, instead of the other *yes* they know is there ... somewhere ... He guards that *yes*, he won't say it. Yet he enacts it. When he drinks saline because they tell him to, that other *yes* is there.

Shortly after they had met for the first time and he had decided to submit to them, László had written:

The play starts
only now in
earnest, the thinking
will come afterward
when we'll have
to face each other
after what we've done.

Rereading this with an hour left of their flight to Amsterdam, they are filled with hope that they will have the opportunity to face László after they have cut him, after they have obliterated his conscious sense of self with pain inflicted with a bamboo cane, after they have made him walk with nails in his shoes, after they have done things to him that are currently beyond the reach of their imagination but whose possibility wafts in their direction the way a stranger's scent passes under their nose as they walk down the tight aisle of the plane.

They want to think with him while looking at the dark bruises on his body that they have made.

Seasonal emerges into the total darkness of 7:00 a.m. on a January morning. László says via WhatsApp:

Oh! Welcome back
to sunny Netherlands!

> *thank you! it is*
> *bleak and my*
> *body is confused.*

Sorry to hear.
Do you have company
to help you through?

> *no :)*
> *does company help*
> *in your experience?*

They don't say how much they are enjoying being alone in their apartment. That they had promised themself the pleasure of their dildo on the endless nothingness that was twenty-three hours of air travel.

Even the dead need
help to move
between worlds, why
wouldn't the living

need that a
thousand times more?

Where does he get these turns of phrase? they ask their kitchen. If he was a student in their creative writing course, they would suspect him of plagiarism. Later, he will send them his writing about a trip to Jerusalem, when they had asked to read more of his academic work. *I want you to know what I think about life, about the world,* he will say, his hands in his pockets, *not what I think about the internet.*

For now, the help they need to move between worlds is not in the form of academic talk about the effect of algorithms on marginalized populations in the United States. This is what is bringing László to Utrecht tonight. They don't say *I want to stay home to write notes about you and masturbate,* knowing he would cherish this information, but also because they do not know how to speak this truth. They don't say *I will make myself come thinking about nails in your shoes.* They say, with a different kind of honesty:

> *i am worried*
> *about my stamina*
> *and concentration.*

You know where to
find me if you need
company and are
awake. :)

The Lost Pencil

Seasonal gets back into the rhythm of the life they are trying to build in Europe. They work, socialize, and continue their correspondence with László. The two of them are trying to understand how Seasonal's dick fits into the power exchange. They had both thought they were playing with pain, punishment, and restraint, but the dildo has expanded the interaction in ways they struggle to account for. László offers:

There was a genius
turn-of-the-century
Hungarian writer, with
some really original
ideas, Karinthy.

One of his lines
that survived as an
idiom is the following:

I had a dream,
in which I was two
cats, and I was
playing with each other.

Seasonal has an intuitive understanding of what he is trying to say
about desire via Karinthy, but they are unable to put it into words
to confirm it. This two-catness slips away from them, as their chat
with him becomes mired in more mundane problems of how to make
room for fantasy within reality. They are unable to find time to meet;
their schedules don't align, but Seasonal also starts to have the feeling
that László is stalling. They find the constant scheduling conversations frustrating and deeply tedious. The question of when and how to
meet never seems to find a resolution without what Seasonal feels are
unnecessarily long and too-detailed descriptions of László's respon-
sibilities. They wonder if he is trying to make it clear that being a
married family man is *really very hard*. Mostly, they try to store up
the energy from the frustration for the next time they will have his
testicles in the palm of their hand. But they also admit to themself
that people can be very boring.

After one particularly frustrating exchange in which László explains he
must travel back and forth between Amsterdam, Paris, and Brussels over
several weeks in order to pursue more funding to study the internet,
Seasonal proposes a new solution—why don't they just meet him in one
of these locations? László quickly agrees, and so after over a month of
back and forth, Seasonal boards the high-speed train from Rotterdam
to Brussels. They will arrive at 21:00 and leave at 14:00 the next day.
A seventeen-hour date. When they spoke via video chat to finalize the
arrangements, László suggested that perhaps they could visit the comics

museum in Brussels together. Seasonal is not sure that would be good use of their time or talents. They are preoccupied with the new challenge: they are meeting him without the home-ground advantage. This is terrifying and interesting. What can their dom self muster in a foreign room? How can they possess a space they do not know?

Perhaps they should tell him he cannot enter the room until they arrive? Then they could discover the room together. Or should they invite him to make the room the way he likes it? These questions preoccupy them as the train pulls out of Rotterdam Centraal Station, heading south.

The small red suitcase sitting above Seasonal's head in the luggage rack contains:
the cuffs and padlocks they bought for László in Australia
the double dildo and lubricant
the harness for the dildo
the piece of rope László presented to them
the silk scarf their mother bought them in Turkey, which they use to take his sight
a kettle
loose-leaf black tea and a tea infuser
a double-chamber glass teacup
roasted almonds
a 100-gram bar of Green & Black's milk chocolate with sea salt
earplugs
silk pants
period underwear

When they realized this morning the blood was coming, they cursed it. And then thought, *Yes, good, this will add something.*

They messaged László:

how do you feel
about menstrual
blood?

When I was younger
I really loved
the bloodbath.

Nowadays the enthusiasm
is gone but I
don't have any
aversions
So no worries
:)

They smile at the idea of his young self in love with *the bloodbath.*

László had said as they were finalizing the arrangements that he no longer needed to evaluate each of their encounters … he was *in*. Seasonal has no idea what this means but they are becoming more comfortable with the deep voice inside them that tells them they want to own László. Destroy him. Cut him. Hit him with bamboo.

They doubt he can be owned.

But they will have fun trying.

Seasonal has instructed László to message them when he arrives at the hotel in Brussels. He is scheduled to arrive a few hours before them, on a train from Paris. They have told him they have instructions for him regarding how he should wait for them. They are undecided as to what these instructions actually are. They are tired, keen to see him and feel his warm body. Power exchange or no, the intimacy and sense of peace that comes from him will be welcome.

Looking out the window, Seasonal knows the train has left the Netherlands and entered Belgium—the houses are less tidy, the architecture more unruly, the font is rounder on the signs at the train stations the Thalys speeds through. They watch the winter darkness stream by, but mostly they are looking at their own reflection in the window because the train carriage is brightly lit and the outside is deep winter darkness. The face looking back at them is serious. Determined. The two vertical thinking lines that sit parallel between their heavy eyebrows are deeply furrowed. Those two lines frame the thing they know and cannot know.

László has reported he wants to be able to say *yes* to them. Seasonal hears this as a bounded wish.

What is a wish? László could not say *yes* when they met him. Seasonal taught him to say it using the tools of willfulness and inventive punishment. Now he professes that he *wants* to say it. But he has also installed someone—his partner—who can override his *yes* with her *no*. Clearly he likes to be restrained by more than cuffs and rope. Seasonal routinely turns their mind to this paradox, and the train ride offers another opportunity to mull it over. That László wants to occupy a position of wishing to say *yes* in a context in which another can nullify the *yes* with a *no*, thereby making his statement meaningless, does not seem to be a paradox to him. He seems so clear in his desire for it. It is not the muddled wishing of someone who does not know what they want—the inarticulate, unfocused wishing of the Russian or the Sound Engineer or even the Parisian, who want to visit Seasonal's desire like the tourists that walk the Red Light District of Amsterdam looking at the bodies of the women in the windows with the same gaze they use on the globally available clothes in the *H&M* and *The Night Watch* in the Rijksmuseum.

When László wishes, his voice has a ring of specificity, truth, desire that Seasonal recognizes. It has something of the future in it. It rings like a large porcelain bowl.

Their eyes rest, unfocused, on the window. They are doggedly working the paradox as though it is a terrible knot of electric cables that they have been given the task of untying. Perhaps—they think, trying a new approach to the knot—the position he wishes from is forged in an agreement about desire and intimacy and partnership between two Hungarians which is as unknowable to them as the Hungarian language. They open a web browser on their phone and load Google Translate. They type "desire" into the left-hand box, and select Hungarian as the target language. A word appears:

vágy

Google—which they know from their Dutch lessons is entirely unreliable—tells them this word can mean "desire, wish, thirst, eagerness, cupidity." (*Cupidity*, the internet tells them, *is greed for money or possessions*.) But when they reverse the translation, *vágy* becomes "obsession."

For "wish," Google offers *szeretnék*, but when that is reversed it becomes the phrase "I want."

They marvel at how language morphs and shifts in this rudimentary algorithmic tool. There is no solid ground to be found here. They wonder briefly about the inside of László's head, guts, erogenous zones; how do English and Hungarian intermingle there?

Seasonal suspects László is wishing for a way to get back to the first time he achieved the satisfaction of his desire by saying *yes*. Was that when he got up from the bathroom floor in Seoul and phoned them? No, it was a long time ago, back in his early experiences of need and frustration and desire and satisfaction and longing, when he did not fully know the cruel nature of the divide between himself and the world. It is back there in history, in a language, geography, and culture that is unknowable to Seasonal. He said *yes* then, and he was lost in bliss and comfort and safety.

They are no closer to untying the cables, and their head is starting to hurt. But perhaps they have made a kind of progress. They have discerned two different cables in the mess. The paradox of László's bounded wish is constituted twice over in a beautiful yet incomprehensible sign system, culture, history that produces a poet who says: *I had a dream, in which I was two cats, and I was playing with each other.* It is geographical and highly personal. It is so remote to Seasonal they do not even know how to adopt a position from which to admire it. All they can do is acknowledge they will always be clueless. They will always be the stranger he wants.

They alight from the Thalys and walk toward the hotel in Brussels. Seasonal pauses to smoke a cigarette. Why do they relish the position of being the stranger hearing a bounded wish? Why do they want to listen to an attractive married man say with true longing and innocent desire in his voice that he wants to say *yes* to them, knowing full well there is a woman behind him who can say *no*, who can crack the porcelain bowl?

Sometimes they wonder if they are being what an Australian would derisively describe as a *fucking idiot* (pronounced *farkin'*, very long in the *a*). They can hear the phrase spoken in their mind sometimes when they are chatting with him in WhatsApp, or walking to meet him. It comes in the strong working-class, rural Australian accent of their family, which Seasonal has lost over the years because their life has led them to spend more time talking to non-Australians than to Australians. They make eye contact with themself in the train station window, and they can hear the high-pitched nasal judgement: *Jesus, Seasonal, what are ya doin'? Ah ya a farkin' idiot?*

Sometimes being called a *farkin' idiot* can act as a warning: *You'd be a farkin' idiot to touch that*, someone might say to you as you approach the thing that could deliver a high-voltage shock. But mostly it comes after the fact, when the mistake has been made and someone wants to shame you for your action and its results. When they want to pass judgement on whatever led you to do that thing. When they want to tell you that your desire to touch the thing makes no sense to them and they think it is dangerous.

No, they say simply to the voice suggesting they may be a fucking idiot. (Is it male? They can't tell.) Something in their instinct says that László's wish is indeed a paradox and will most likely, then, be true. There is something undeniably real and compelling in his wish, and in being the person he voices it to. When you translate "yes" into Hungarian, Google gives you the word *igen*. When you reverse the translation, *igen* becomes "yes."

Saying *igen* to his desire still routinely eludes László. Yesterday, having agreed to meet in Brussels, Seasonal had given him an easy question to say *yes* to. They gave him an opportunity to have his wish.

He did not say *yes*.

He said: *Will do.*

They told him to *try again.* That they were disappointed and perplexed. It was 12:40 a.m. They sighed heavily and put the phone on the bedside table and went to sleep.

At 9:00 a.m. the next morning, he responded: *yes.*

Extinguishing their cigarette and moving toward the taxi stand, Seasonal opens WhatsApp and types the instructions.

take a shower

dry yourself

*dress yourself, if
you will be more
comfortable*

lie in the dark,
or find somewhere
to sit

wait there until
i arrive.

An hour later, László meets Seasonal on the street outside Hôtel Le Dôme, a three-star hotel that spans the corner of a once-grand street in the east of Brussels. They look at each other nervously. Seasonal lights a cigarette to calm their nerves and offers an observation.

Well, we are out of comfort zones.

Yes, László says easily, smiling, relieved.

The two walk up two flights of stairs with threadbare green carpet and enter the large room with a long line of windows along the street. They lie on the two hard beds, in their jeans and black T-shirts. Looking at each other, trying to find a way across the tentativeness that defines the first few hours of each of their meetings They talk about the power exchange. Seasonal tries to describe how they are using their sexual attraction to László to reroute the gendered, socially acceptable responses they have to being annoyed. They explain to László that expressing their annoyance feels incredibly arrogant and unkind. The night before, when he had texted *Will do* instead of *yes*, they had forced themself not to make excuses for him, and to say *try again*. László admitted that he knew, the minute he typed *Will do*, that he had said the wrong thing, but that he had decided not to correct it. He smiles as he tells this story.

Fuck you! they say laughing.

He likes his joke, but there is something more serious underlying the insult. The longer László withholds these small but important gestures of acquiescence, the longer he makes Seasonal wait to progress. On the one hand, they have to respect the way he is playing the game—the power of his defenses against submission, against his annihilation—on the other, they feel like saying in exasperation *I can only stay at level one with you for so long.*

I don't think you want a true submissive, László says, teasingly. *It would be too boring for you, no challenge.*

They know László likes being a challenge. He is good at it.

You are right, they admit. *As I said when we met the first time, the will to master, the challenge of learning someone and gaining their submission, is at least 80 percent of the pleasure to me.*

I want to break the horse I ride, they think, but don't say. Instead, Seasonal tells László they want to kiss him, and he says:

Do it.

But they make them both wait, by telling him how disappointed they were that they could not get him to make love to them through the phone while they were in Australia.

I know, he says, *you were too far.*

They almost say, *I could reach you in Seoul, your powers clearly have less reach than mine.* They realize later that they should have; they know this is the voice of arrogance they need to cultivate.

He begins a segue by asking them if they have read a particular contemporary novel he has just started.

Oh great, they say, leaning across the gap between the two beds, *start talking to me about literature, then I will kiss you to make you shut up.*

Being out of their comfort zones brings out their willingness to be tender with each other: they take their time with their eyes, their mouths, their hands. Hands on necks and faces, in hair, hands moving outside jeans and T-shirts. Smiling. Pausing. But also the slow build, the body's reaction to what might now be thought of—as this is their third time together—as a return. Or at least, the relieving immediate anticipation that when more is wanted, more will be had.

They enfold each other, and as their T-shirts are removed, Seasonal realizes the threshold that is approaching.

Have you marked your body already?

He smiles, pleased. He likes that they know he is capable of disobedience.

No.

Good. I thought I better check, given you like to do it without telling me.

His slow intake of his breath tells them he likes this too.

They roll László on his back and straddle him.

We are approaching an important decision, they announce.

He looks up at them, open-faced, interest piqued.

How far are you allowed to go without a mark on your body?

They enjoy this question together. Smiling, kissing, the pleasure of light and firm skin contact.

Seasonal has no interest in making their sexuality, their body, something someone has to earn. This model of feminine arrogance, of holding the body at a distance until a series of tests have been satisfied, is merely a compensation for the assumed surrender that must follow, and the near-constant state of disempowerment that attends the female body in the patriarchy. (In the morning, over tea, László will tell them that he does not like accounts of anything that are too structural, they *downplay the role of human agency and resistance.* They think: *How lucky, to be able to choose whether or not structures should be given attention.*) They would fuck unmarked László any day of the week. But if they do, they have to care about his pleasure, and Seasonal is not sure they want to do that.

They talk and smile and handle each other through this conundrum. They feel their way toward and around what might be the difference between fucking with and without the mark. Enjoying the interstitial space.

What would be the difference?

If you wear the mark, I won't care about your pleasure.

He dilates with anticipation.

I will wear it then.

Before you do, is there anything you want?

László takes more time with their body.

I do not want anything from you that I cannot have when I am wearing the mark, he says definitively. *You can remind me of that later when I am wearing it.*

He stands and moves toward his brown satchel on the floor.

Seasonal lies back and marinates in anticipation. They hear him rummaging in his bag. He turns on a small lamp on the desk and continues looking. His body language changes from the long-limbed fluidity of arousal to a rigid anxiety. Seasonal says nothing and lets time do its work, as they did when they ran the timer before making him drink saline. The rummaging becomes more frantic. And then he turns to them, his brow knitted in concern.

It is not lost. I carry it with me always, along with your letters, but I cannot find it now.

Seasonal sits up but maintains a still, cool silence. In ordinary life, now is the moment they would join the search, begin to smooth over the situation. Instead, they hold back, stepping away from the natural inclination to help and toward the rage that is blooming in their chest.

They concentrate on setting their features and look at him.

It is not lost, I just can't find it. Desperation and anxiety thin his normally deep, calm voice. *I understand the gravity of the situation.*

I would like to see you tip the contents of that bag on the floor, Seasonal says coolly.

He doesn't do it.

A thread of tension takes hold between them. László wants to resolve the situation, move on, as soon as possible. Seasonal wants to explore this unexpected opportunity to stew in their frustration, to feel how it takes hold in their body, and how it might shift what they do with and through their body with him. They lean backward and try to resist his attempts to draw them into the dilemma. They try to embrace the cold detachment that is crystalizing their usually open and amenable personality into something else, something new.

László abandons his search and tells them he wants to mark his body anyway. Seasonal holds out as long as they can, and then they relent. They are trying to save face because they could not find the move that would result in them slapping his face, or throwing him out of the room. They let him find an alternative because they are frozen by their rage and disappointment, rather than feeling agile in it. László

retrieves a pen from his satchel, and Seasonal is immediately horrified by what is about to happen. A degraded, meaningless act in ink.
Seasonal knows it is not done for them, even though László thinks it
is. It is done out of an appeal to ritual. It brings them no pleasure to
see the mark he makes on his wrist. It is the mark of their failure, it is
the mark of his carelessness. It is a mark of desire, but, they think as he
places the cap back on the ballpoint pen, *We would have been better off
to just fuck without it.*

They are tired, and their shared uncertainty about the moment as it
unfolds turns Seasonal into a failed dom. Together they return to the
bed, and return to their shared interest in pain: they grip each other,
using hands and pressure on testicles, labia, nipples, skin. The tenderness of their touch before the discovery of the missing pencil returns
easily and they forget and escape together. All the tools of BDSM that
Seasonal packed remain in the red suitcase.

In the morning, as Seasonal snoozes and László snores, they realize
what they have to say when he wakes up: *I have a question. I want to
play with you before I leave today, what do you say?*

They manage to get the question in shortly after he wakes up, but he
does not say *yes* or *no.* He says *OK.* He acknowledges the question
kindly, openly. He thinks on it. But then he is talking about breakfast,
about a phone call he has to make at 10:00 a.m. He tries to leave
the bed and gets caught in their body. He lies with his head on their
crotch, his arms entangled in their legs. This taking of comfort, of
pleasure, catches Seasonal off guard. They do not understand how this
is the same man who lost the pencil.

Looking down at his peaceful face resting on their navel, an image László had sent them comes into Seasonal's mind. It is of the male body. Naked, on his knees, hands tied behind his back, head in the sheets, face hidden. This is how they have to position him for losing the pencil. If he consents to play, they will position him this way and then they will sodomize him.

As talk of breakfast unfolds, László's *OK* hanging in the air, it dawns on Seasonal that this will not happen before his business lunch. They go out and walk and find croissants, and László tells them about the sex toy he wants to design that will use body sensors to edge its user. He talks about the moment when everything clicks into place when you are being edged; he thinks it is mind-expanding.

It sounds like an instrument of torture, they say walking the dreary streets of Brussels.

His laugh is generous.

Having barely survived your edging, the idea of that machine makes me nervous.

László claims he *is not edging* them. Seasonal wonders what he *is* doing.

They return to the hotel room and László leaves for his lunch meeting at the funding body that may want to give him two million euros to study the internet. He is distracted, anxious, as he buttons his dark-blue peacoat over a deep-red shirt.

Bye, he says awkwardly.

Bye, Seasonal echoes.

Seasonal writes in the hotel room. Through the paper-thin walls, they hear an accomplished clarinet player practicing. After two hours, the front desk calls and demands Seasonal leave the room so that the rough sheets and single bath towel can be replaced. They prepare to decamp to the lobby. It is an hour before their train leaves for Amsterdam, and they wonder if they should just disappear. They get into the lift with their laptop, their reading glasses propped on the top of their head. As the lift door opens on the ground floor, there stands László, a *Visitor* badge still pinned to his coat. He smiles, relieved.

They sit together side by side on the 1980s grey leather couch in the lobby, their feet on the coffee table.

Have you thought about my question?

Yes. His eyes widen in the way they have come to recognize as anticipation. *Yes. I would like to play with you this afternoon.*

So I will book a later train.

They open their laptop. The 20:44 train will do. That buys six hours.

I admire your freedom and flexibility, he says as he watches them book and pay for the ticket. *I appreciate it very much.*

I am going to make you pay for forgetting the pencil.

His open expression is tinged with gravity.

I am afraid.

They show him the picture he sent them. The man on his knees, his face in the sheets.

This is where we will start.

Did I send you that? His face is a mix of incredulity and arousal. *Now I feel real fear.*

He smiles nervously. *Is it too late to back out?*

They grin at each other.

They decide that lunch is probably a good idea, and over ersatz Belgian ramen they agree it is clearly Seasonal's job, as the dom, to lead them through the impasse of the lost pencil and the fissure it has created in their fledging power exchange. They have to punish László, and they have to set the scene—or reset the scene—for the power exchange to regain its proper imbalance. They compare their experiences of last night: for László, the marking of his body is still important, regardless of the implement he uses to do it; they disagree.

I have carried the pencil with me everywhere I go since you gave it to me. I carry it with my passport, which I also carry with me at all times.

This shocks and impresses them.

So the pencil is a symbol of freedom to you?

He nods a quick, boyish nod.

They had thought that perhaps the time of the pencil was over, but the idea that it is with him as a symbol of freedom softens Seasonal. They have their freedom, they enact it every day. László, perhaps, needs a pencil and a passport in his bag to remind him of its existence. They feel proud and moved that they have been able to create this experience for him. It confirms their investment in the pencil as the object that connects them to him; that is a symbol of their agreement.

I took it from my bag over the Christmas–New Year period because I was traveling a lot and I did not want to lose it. It is in Amsterdam. I will confirm for you as soon as I locate it.

They notice he does not say *home*, but *Amsterdam*.

Have you been traveling since then believing and feeling like it was with you?

Yes.

As they watch László eat soup, Seasonal thinks about the letter he wrote announcing his departure from Hungary, about all the writing they've been doing together in WhatsApp, the writing Seasonal has been compelled to do on the Notes app on their phone, the writing they do with each other's body, with eyeliner pencils, and the writing they are about to embark on now with cuffs and a dildo They realize the bond that is forming between them. Each wants to turn their anger and disappointment into something legible and worthwhile. Into the authority to choose their own path.

As they leave the restaurant with László, Seasonal asks:

How is your fear?

Settling into a hard-on, he replies, standing tall.

As they walk back to the hotel they ask László if he would like to know what is coming when he enters the room. He says *yes*. They tell him he can take as long as he needs to mark his body. Once he has, he will be immobilized like the man in the picture, and then they will see how long he should stay that way.

László's submission is only possible if he knows it brings the other pleasure. He kneels before them on the thin carpet of the Hôtel Le Dôme, pen in hand, and asks them:

What pleasure does my submission bring you?

Seasonal confesses to the long game, that they are working toward his full submission. They don't say that they want to own him. But they do say:

In this moment, I find it astonishing that someone I respect as much as I respect you is prepared to surrender their will to me.

He writes *FREE* on his shoulder. They take the pen from his hand and add *MY*—and—*DOM*. They tell him to undress.

Soon, László is standing naked with his hands cuffed behind his back.

I am afraid, he says. *Can I ask you to kiss me?*

Seasonal withholds the kiss and gently leads him toward the bed. They arrange László's body in the position of the man in the image. Cuffed hands at the base of his spine. Face in the pillow, his buttocks raised high. Seasonal watches his eyes fill with struggle and fear. His face sets in determination. Total presence. He briefly searches their face with frantic eyes, and then retreats into himself. He looks to them, to himself, to them again. His face is flushed, the muscles in his neck stand high.

Can I touch you? they ask, watching the struggle.

They cradle his sex in their hand. He begins to change. As they slowly tighten their grip, and draw from him slow, deep sounds of surrender, Seasonal remembers a fragment of their discussion of the male body from the week before.

*Do I sense correctly
that you have a
specific interest in
power over the
male (body?), not
just simply the
other, or just the
body?*

yes

the male body
is amazing (sex,
pleasure, smell, taste,
visual aesthetics,
how it interacts with
my body, comportment)
but as someone
socialized as a
woman, the male
body has also
been a signifier
of threat: i have
been socialized to
fear it.

that is gender/
patriarchy

how do i mediate
my powerful desire
and interest in
it, my desire
to explore it
in its fullness,
in the context
of normative gender
relations?

those normative
relations position

(213)

my body and
desire as passive
and receptive, as
responsive but not
active

and i have been
socialized to believe
that my desire for
the male body will
put me at risk

am i making
sense?

Now it is László who must bear the risk of Seasonal's desire for the male body. Their left hand slowly turns into a vice, the soft orbs of his testes yielding to the pressure of questions Seasonal does not know how to ask. Maintaining the pressure with their left hand, they put the index and middle fingers of their right hand into their mouth, down to the knuckle, and make them slick with spit. They do the same with their thumb, and then run their thumb with a slow force around László's rim. He is wet. They place a firm pressure with their thumb against the knot of skin that is the threshold to his need. His deep moan shifts upward, he emits a siren's call. Seasonal feels him soften and open under their touch. They release some pressure from his testicles and pull them down toward the bed, suspending him between two forces: one down, the other wanting to come in. They gently slip inside him, feeling the welcome his body offers their thumb. They replace it with the pressure of two fingers that have been in their mouth again. They succumb to their curiosity about him, plunging into his body.

These opening moves lead to a pleasing long tangle of hands and fingers, teeth and tongues. Questions, limit testing, responses and exclamations. Seasonal is learning how to come inside, rather than welcome. Time bends. Afterward, Seasonal asks:

How was it?

It did not feel like punishment. It felt like a gift, László responds dreamily. *I am looking for a male lover like you. Generous, open, giving. They are hard to find.*

Seasonal lies on their back on the hard bed, staring at the ceiling, hands behind their head.

The person who introduced me to the double dildo I fucked you with calls me boy, they admit in the half-light.

That is an entirely inadequate form of address for you. You are so much more than that. It does not capture the multiple dimensions and attitudes that you encompass. László is surprisingly strident. Seasonal finds his indignity endearing.

Let him call you whatever he wants, Seasonal thinks, as they move their hand across László's warm, slack body.

Finally, Seasonal drags themself from the hard mattress to the small bathroom. They need to shower before getting the train. They are losing a significant amount of blood. It is the first twenty-four hours of their menstruation. There is blood on the sheet, on their bodies. It is good blood: deep, dark red. It smells of iron, of life.

They look at their body in the bathroom mirror and there is dried blood smeared all over their vagina and torso. They laugh under the unflattering blueish fluorescent light. Their pale skin reflects a greenish tinge from the mint-colored tiles in the bathroom. *This would be a good image for the Sound Engineer to catch.*

I hope they don't think you murdered someone in here, they say, returning to the room to get dressed and looking at the large bloodstain on the bedsheet next to László's body.

I am from Eastern Europe, he says casually, *they will think I was preparing my own meat.*

Seasonal packs and leaves.

have you found
your pencil?

Not yet

i want to put
something in your
shoe

Do you want
to talk?

                                       have you found
                                           the pencil?

Not at home
I will now
check the uni

In the afternoon
I would like to
talk to you
if possible

When László calls just after 4:00 p.m. on a Tuesday, Seasonal is standing on their balcony drinking tea, trying not to smoke. He is back in Brussels, this time for a conference, and as they greet each other on the phone Seasonal immediately detects a deep shade of dread in his voice. Their clitoris hears it too.

I must tell you I cannot find the pencil.

Profuse apologizing follows. But it is the fear they can hear in his voice that makes the phone call worth it—not the words. They laugh at his incompetence. They laugh as the rage he so wishes to see flashes white across their retina and incredulity floods their central nervous system. They are shaking with fury. The pencil has paid unexpected dividends. *He can convince a bunch of people in the Dutch Research Council to give him a million euros in research funding,* they think, *but he cannot keep a fifteen-euro eyeliner pencil safe?* They know László has lost the pencil because he is unable to look after their desire. He cannot think of them—he cannot hold them.

He feels truly abject in the face of his failure, he is confused and sorry. The sheet of rage across Seasonal's sight is replaced by the golden light of having orchestrated his humiliation with such a mundane object and simple request.

He wants to know what will happen now.

They tell him to call them tomorrow.

After they hang up they send him a message.

you are intriguing
and frustrating

please come to
our conversation tomorrow
with a clear sense of
when you can be
in a room with me.
i will expect to
be able to ask
you this, and to
get an answer.
ok?

Yes

May I call you
from Brussels after
11:00 p.m. tonight?

by losing the
pencil, you have sent
us back to the
beginning. if you
are prepared to
begin again, to try
again to find your
way to submission
to me then yes,
you can call me.

please confirm you
intend to do so.

Yes, Seasonal, I
would like to continue,
by starting again,
if this is what
is needed.

That night it is a tense negotiation. László wonders *if the pencil is really needed.* Seasonal bristles; he has clearly failed to take any notice of the pleasure it brings them when he uses it. They had worked so hard to communicate this pleasure to him, and the pleasure of hearing his *yes*, and yet these two basic things he cannot give consistent attention. He texts *Will do* or poetic descriptions of what he would like (*to continue by starting again*) when he knows they want a *yes*. He thinks the mark on his body is merely a way for him to say he is ready to be used, that he can stop thinking and be passive, rather than a signal that they have achieved his submission and that he must pay more attention than ever.

But he agrees to change his plans and come to them tomorrow on his return to Amsterdam. He was going to spend the night in Brussels after a long day at the conference, but he will come to Utrecht instead in order to attempt to remedy his mistake.

Seasonal's rage is no longer white. It is a colorless gas that replaces the air in their lungs and the oxygen in their blood. The muscle in their left bicep twitches with the impulse to throw the phone that is the conduit of László's faltering desire and inattention. Their sinus cavity tightens, their shoulders rise like elevators traveling to the penthouse, and their body is taught. Their lower jaw is made of concrete and their teeth ache for the soft flesh of László's chest.

The following day, Seasonal's work passes easily and they teach what feels to them like an interesting and lively class. After work, they shower and send a message:

are you on your
way?

Seasonal is standing in their bedroom, the double dildo inserted, holding their cock in their left hand and thinking of László. They smirk at the delicious incongruity of the situation. He is on his way to them. To offer himself, so that they can use him for their pleasure. His willingness to change his travel plans allows them to continue this process of estrangement from themself, this journey that they find as hard to register on the physical plane as the sixteen thousand five hundred and thirty-seven kilometers from Melbourne to Utrecht. In the months since discovering H had let them go, they have written a new form of transportation, whose velocity is shocking and thrilling. It is powered by a strange amalgam of digital and analog materials, and it appears to be a perpetual propulsion machine.

I just left Antwerp

And I'm anxious
as hell

It is terrible

But I regard it
as already being
part of the exchange

i could share a
picture with you
if that would help

They rest their mobile phone on the chest of drawers, reverse the camera and set the filter to black and white. They select a three-second timer and snap a picture of their groin in the black harness, the prosthetic pointing in profile, their left hand at the base of their cock.

László must be somewhere close to Rotterdam when he messages.

May I ask if
you have any
particular fantasies
attached to you
wearing the male
sex?

oh, have you
forgotten all the
wonderful things i
said to you
before i fucked
you?

No.

you want me
to tell you again?

I feel them on
my body as we
speak

But if you'll allow
me, I'll ask some
questions again and
again

Not because I don't
remember what
you said

But because I'm
interested in how
the answers may
change as we change

so i shall answer
for you now

it is not the
male sex that is
the fantasy, nor
have i ever
fantasized about
wearing it in
the abstract

(226)

(this is one
of the reasons
i know i
am not trans)

i wear it, and
i want to be
with you through
it / with it,

because i caught
a glimpse of your
desire for it
the first time we
met

and i have seen
you when that
desire has been
explored, a little

and i see something
else in you
through this mechanism

this prothesis

that i find
magnetic, attractive,
and
beautiful

(I'm blushing now)

i think these
other things i
see in you
have a role to
play in your
exploration of
submission

and it is your
submission that i
fantasize about :)

László changes trains at Rotterdam to the Intercity service to Utrecht, and keeps typing.

I would like to
tell you something
so that I can
ask if it resonates
with you

I never had a
lover with whom
I felt the same

freedom to explore
my submissive? bottom?
feminine? part of
my personality

(I don't use these
words interchangeably,
but I don't have
one that covers them
all)

So I don't have
the language to
express them in a
way that would
match what I feel
inside

Like hearing music
in my head
without being able
to play it

This is what I
saw in that picture

Time and space
to find the words,

The movements, the silences

*The opportunity, your
help in turning
everything I know
inside out, upside down.*

Seasonal reads these messages sitting in their armchair. The dildo is cleaned, upstairs. They have written a plan in a notebook to prepare for László's arrival:

Ground floor: obedience, sit for forty minutes
First floor: surrender, cuffs
Bedroom: immobilization, denial, cock in mouth

They know they have to hold him through his fear on the train. They ask:

do you have any
sense of why you
have not felt free
to explore your
desire for submission
this freely before?
with others?

Yes

I never fully
trusted my male lovers

Or, to be exact,
I haven't found any
male lover I wanted
to meet a
second/third time

And you are the
first woman I know
who feels herself
comfortable with
a strap-on, and
with a guy so
eager to take it.

When they had fucked the Sound Engineer with their cock a day earlier, he had said a similar thing.

That was a first, he said, impressed.

Your energy with it is really intense. It is really something. It is beautiful.

His smile, too, was different. Seasonal wonders what they are unlocking.

The more I think
about this, the
more complex it gets,

László continues typing from the train.

As there seem to
be a number of
characteristics that
came together this
time.

That you are a
woman (or that
you possess qualities
that I deeply respect
AND associate with
women), that there
is a dick, which,
as an axis, literally
enables turning things
around, your comfort
in wearing it, your
focus on gender
and power

All seem to be
necessary

I am arriving in
Utrecht now

Forty minutes after writing this message, László is sitting at the bottom of the stairs in the narrow vestibule of Seasonal's apartment. He is wearing his work clothes: purple shirt, dark blazer, jeans. The orange floor tiles he sits near are never washed, the threadbare brown carpet on the stairs is held together by dust. A draft comes under the front door.

Seasonal sits upstairs, on the first floor, reading Anne Boyer's poem on the crush and listening to Keith Jarrett.

After twenty minutes they want him. It seems a waste to have him down there for the planned forty minutes. He is sitting on the second step, facing the door. Beside the compost bin.

Would you like to come upstairs? They ask from high above him on the steep Dutch staircase.

Thank you. Yes. I would like to take a shower.

Having recently ridden the trains from Brussels to Utrecht, they understand his need. A shower is not in the plan, but they consent. He disappears upstairs and returns twenty minutes later clean and happy.

They talk. Drink tea. His gaze is wide and intent. The boyish smile is there. The mix of pride and timidity in his stance that they recognize as his desire for submission. He kneels on the rug in front of their chair. They take the cuffs out of a calico bag. He holds out his wrists. They are almost struck dumb by his willingness. Until they see the pride he takes in offering himself to them, and they remember he has no idea what he is doing.

László follows Seasonal upstairs and sees the dildo and the coiled rope on the bed. They tell him to lie down, to keep his clothes on. They tell him to bind his own ankles with the rope. They devour his body language with the rope: the efficient movements of his hands, the decisive gestures he uses to immobilize himself. They take out the blue silk scarf their mother bought them in Turkey. (*It was not cheap,* she had said when giving it to them.) They hold the dildo in one hand and the scarf in the other.

I am going to take your sight. And then you are going to listen to me use this. You cannot touch me.

His disappointment is charged and pointed. They cover his eyes with the scarf and slip the female end of the dildo into their slick cunt. They sigh, they hum. László writhes. He reaches out for them, they push his hand away.

No.

When they release him, he takes the dildo in his mouth and pushes the female end deeper into their need with his hunger.

They smile when he asks them to fuck him. They hear the need in it. They have found the way to make him beg. They have discovered how to make him feel his emptiness, his need, his incompleteness, and instilled in him the belief that the only respite from this hunger is them and their cock.

When he says *please*, Seasonal believes him.

When Seasonal orgasms—watching him turn on the axis—they do not lose their edges. Their edges expand, and László is within them. He belongs to them.

I Want to Be Your Whore

I was not fucked
often enough to
know all the pleasure
being fucked can
bring to me or
to my partner
who fucks me.

but I know this.

seeing the pleasure
on your face
when you fucked
me gave me
immense joy.

and made me
want to give you
more.

it made me want
to be your whore.

It is conference season, and László has flown to Washington, DC, for a conference about the internet. When Seasonal receives this unexpected proposition, they are overcome with a desire to hear these words.

say it.

They hurriedly send the message before getting on their bicycle to go to work. They are absorbed in the workday: students, colleagues, questions of whether or not literature still matters and if so how. As they leave the university building and walk toward their bicycle, buttoning their coat against the blistering north wind, they finally have time to check their phone. There is a sound file waiting for them. They cycle home quickly and listen. At the beginning of the file, they hear the chatter of dozens of indistinguishable voices in a large open space, and then László begins to speak. His speech has the fast, confident rhythm of his everyday voice:

I am standing in a lobby in the middle of a conference, and I am very ...

His pace slows. The realization of what he is about to say, what he wants to say, that he is about to speak his desire standing there amongst the Americans dawns on him and he changes to the voice they have come to know better, the voice he is trying to find and use

with them, the voice he used when he said *I would like that* the first
day they met.

*... it's a very strange feeling ... to be among people and actually say that
I want to be your whore ... I want ... to feel ... the weight of what this
sentence and me saying this means ... I want to be your whore, Seasonal.*

The *s* at the beginning of *sentence* is elongated. He slips on it like a
footpath which has suddenly frozen. The naming, the admission. He
has said it. *I want to be your whore.*

Seasonal's response to this message is immediate. They are ravenous. They go to their bedroom and lie on the bed. They conjure him, his body as a question, as a need that only they can meet. The phone pings; he asks to see their desire.

They insert the dildo and put their left hand at the base of their cock. The kneel over the phone and snap a picture of their torso and crotch. Their body looms large over the lens—the angle places the viewer underneath them. They put a black-and-white filter on the image and send it.

this is me.
right now. thinking
of you asking
me to fuck
you. and telling
you i will
because you are
my whore.

please remember the
sound i make
when the female
end enters my
body. i made
it just now.
because of how
wet you made me.

it is also important
that it is you
who utters these
words.

when you say
" will fuck you
because you are
my whore"

i hear the words
themselves, with
all the horror they
carry.

i hear you
saying them as
a woman, twisting
them, appropriating
them, subliming them

i hear them
uttered by a queer
person, speaking
from a fluid, non-
binary position.

i hear them
as a masculine
man, as a slut,
as a bisexual
person

and i hear them
from someone i
believe has the
strength to guide
me through this
landscape

:)

Ten days later, László is home from the United States. He has caught a virus while traveling and withdraws for several weeks. Seasonal does not know how to reach him. They settle into their rhythm. They enter psychoanalysis to try to recover from the sudden loss of H. They supervise the research projects of some bright, hopeful students and remember they are no longer young. They struggle through the long, dark weeks wondering if the sun will ever shine again. They meet an Iranian composer via the dating app. His lean body is bristling with muscle, and he has a brisk and decisive nod they find admirable. The first time they have sex, Seasonal lays on their stomach and he covers their entire body with his. His hand on the back of their neck, on their cheek, and every muscle in their body turns soft under his touch and the weight of his presence.

Do you see now, he asks quietly in their ear as he pauses on their threshold, *how much I like you?*

As he enters them, Seasonal realizes his intention.

The next day, wandering alone on the lowest floor of the Rijksmuseum, Seasonal finds the violence that was missing in the frescoes in Florence. A Venetian fresco from 1425 has found its way to Amsterdam. It depicts the martyrdom of Saint Lawrence, who was roasted on a fire for his sins. His pale-white skin lies on top of a long metal grate, under which a fire glows in sharp red. Tiny flames rise above the metal, like the fringe of a magic carpet, and lick his pristine flesh. Lawrence, his stomach bared to the fire, looks upward to the bearded face of God above him. Lawrence faces God with bliss and calm while his body burns. His hands together in prayer, he looks at peace and thankful.

In the same room, Seasonal gazes at a complex scene titled *The Holy Kinship*, painted in 1495 in Haarlem. It is set inside a medieval church and depicts the blood relation between key figures of the Biblical story. Mary and Jesus are front and center, of course, but behind them an executioner's body twists as he swings the sword, about to behead a kneeling, blindfolded victim on top of the altar. Victim and murderer are dressed in resplendent gold robes, and the executioner's dark hair, long moustache, and curved blade indicate that the source of violence comes from outside the city. Is the beheading really happening on the altar, or is it a statue inside the church? It is unclear. No one is looking at the scene of violence; they all face forward, giving their attention to the arrangement of Christ's bloodline. The only person facing the beheading is an altar boy, in white robes, who maneuvers a candle snuffer that is attached to an extraordinarily long pole. It crosses just in front of the executioner's raised arms.

Ten years later, still in Haarlem or perhaps in Amsterdam, *The Martyrdom of Saint Lucy* is painted on a panel which forms part of an altar dedicated to the saint. Lucy is also aflame—but she is dressed, and standing on top of a cluster of logs from which pale-yellow flames leap. A Roman executioner raises one leg and thrusts the tip of his sword into her jugular notch. One hand below the handle steadies the sword's aim, the other drives the sword from the end of the handle. Behind her, a man sits as though doing the splits on the ground, in bright-white tights. He pumps small handheld bellows, to feed the fire of Lucy's immolation. Lucy's hands are folded in prayer, and she looks calmly down. Her perfect pink frock has not yet caught fire, nor has the blow from the Roman yet sent her tumbling.

Throughout the museum, there are beheadings, whippings, people restrained by rope, people in stocks. On the back of a diptych portrait, a cross stands emitting a magnetic field which suspends two floating hands, two floating feet—all with the stigmata—and the sacred heart. The body has departed, leaving only the symbols of its suffering behind.

In László's absence, Seasonal has time to look.

The following week, it is a Wednesday afternoon and the sun has finally emerged. Spring is arriving. Seasonal walks in the center of Amsterdam, away from the central train station. They are on their way to teach a graduate course on digital life writing. They will present their theory of the selfie—which is that we do not yet know what it is. Walking down Spuistraat, a flash of glossy red catches their attention. The immaculately presented women in the windows. Further along the street, empty windows stand. "Red rooms for rent / Kamer te huur."

The room is below the pavement. To see László, you would have to be looking down, not at eye height, where you would see bike stores, coffee shops, or the signs for a notary's office. The small space is tiled floor-to-ceiling in utilitarian white tiles. A sink with a tap sits underneath a large oval mirror on the back wall. A clear plastic chair—like those favored in the tiny rooms of Italian and French hotels—is angled to face the larger part of the window, affording the best view from the street. But he would be forbidden to sit there. He will have been told to kneel. His kneecaps would be white, bearing the force of his sizable frame. He would not be able to bring himself to face the street. He would like to show his pride and shame to the feet of the stoned tourists and the beleaguered students hurrying toward their classes in the University of Amsterdam humanities building down the street. But he would struggle. Only the dark hair on the top of his head would be visible.

Sitting across the street, beside a cluster of British lads rolling their third joint, Seasonal would watch him. They would expand with hope that he will find the courage to lift his eyes. No one will want him if they cannot see his face.

They would be relieved when they see him take a deep breath and raise his head. Determination would darken his features. It would seem impossible that this face knows a boyish grin, the spark of sharp intellect, the ready smile. His jaw would be a hard line. Watching, Seasonal would imagine they hear his teeth grinding, over the gentle continuous sound of the bikes in the two bike lanes, and the low, broad discussion of the lads. He would take the middle distance as his focus point. His eyes set straight, his cuffed wrists held still in front of his simple black cotton underwear. His right hand cupping his left in a light, curled caress.

Framed by the wooden window in a building hundreds of years old, the red light glowing faintly on his skin against the sunshine, he would look spectacular.

On the way back to Utrecht on the train, Seasonal does some research on their phone. The Dutch AIDS council advises that a window prostitute can expect to pay between €80 and €120 for a part-day rental of a window and room. The price does not include the provision of bedding, heating, water, condoms, sex toys, or advertisements.

In the pragmatic Dutch style, the AIDS council outlines the pros and cons of being a *raamprostitutie.* The advantages are:
You work independently
You determine your own prices
You determine your own working hours
You can choose your own customers
You decide how to get your customers

The disadvantages of working the window include:
You have less direct protection
Competition is fierce in a window area
You are open and exposed, including to family, friends, and acquaintances
Tourists see you as an interesting photo for home and Facebook

Seasonal sends László a brief message, admitting they had imagined him in a window today. He responds:

I have been entertaining
the idea of standing
in the window for
some time, but I
was never brave
enough to take the
concrete steps.

The AIDS council advises that the going rate for a fuck (*neuken*) or a blowjob (*pijpen*) is around €50.

Seasonal walks home through the quiet city. They knew, intuitively, that he wanted to be in a window. He wants everything to be taken from him, he wants to be overwhelmed, *overpowered*. Forced. He wants the drive to come from them and to be helpless in the face of it. He wants to be annihilated against his will. He wants someone who will ignore his fear and take everything from him, and in so doing give him the experience of being defeated. Desolate. Without culpability. Seasonal knows László wants to burn in a righteousness that comes from a powerful, external source, like the figures conjured by long-dead painters centuries before.

But the submission Seasonal seeks is the opposite of this. Seasonal knows that taking, that ignoring the fear of the other and over-whelming that other with their need, will not free power from its ossified state. To overwhelm László in this way is merely to stage the same old practices of domination. Seasonal seeks something else. Something impossible, perhaps. They are seeking an exchange, not to take something from someone who pretends to hold on to it tightly in order to conceal the shame of their desire. Seasonal feels this searching for something else deep in their body, but when they turn their mind to finding the words to describe it, they are blank. All they know is what they know: that this other form of power would bring no shame through defeat. The other would not burn to ashes in blissful mar-tyrdom, but would become a source of fire themself. Defeat would be a pleasure of surrender, of giving over without damage or violence. This submission and its corresponding domination would involve sharing, joyful complicity and cooperation, not a reification of polarization.

In the face of László's need and ongoing resistance, Seasonal tries not to feel too stupid for knowing and wanting this.

Baszdüh

László has recovered from his virus, and Seasonal asks if they can meet for a walk. They arrange to meet on a Wednesday afternoon. Seasonal looks at the man waiting for them near the river and realizes they know nothing about him except some of his deepest fears, the sound he makes when he surrenders to his desire, and that he is careless with objects. It is the first time they've met without the intention of negotiating something within the power exchange. They are meeting each other with the faces they show the world, as ordinary people, who want to stretch their legs together.

They walk in silence. The afternoon is cold and they follow the Amstel River from Amstel Station toward the center of town. They are unsure how to proceed. The confusion is not uncomfortable. It is, in fact, the cornerstone their relationship. They come together to not know, but also to pursue the knowledge each of them has held alone, as a shameful secret. Each of them is trying to find new sentences, to say things they never thought they would say to another living person, speaking from and about the troublesome point where body, personality, intellect, and feeling collide—or diverge.

I have spent forty-four years not speaking my desires. It is going to take some time to undo, László says as the two of them stop to greet a calico cat who is guarding a narrow houseboat. Seasonal watches him as he bends down to offer his hand to the cat. They wonder what he has spent forty-four years speaking about with his friends, his lovers, his partner. Seasonal is adjusting to the long pauses he requires. He is slow and contemplative. Glacial.

A few days later, László sends a message. He is meeting with lawyers who want to know about the internet at a conference in the city of Tilburg, which lies in the Catholic south of the Netherlands. He has rented a small house via Airbnb, and he invites Seasonal to join him. The two of them have been sending messages about beams, beatings, whoring.

As Seasonal packs their bag, they send him a message asking if there's anything in particular they should bring with them.

I would like to
ask you to fuck
me

The place is an
old house.
It has a beam
just at the right
height.

Arriving in Tilburg, Seasonal is immediately looking for cigarettes. László sends a message to say he is on the way to meet them at the train station.

> *i am already*
> *here*

As they look up from sending this message they see him. He is wearing black pants, a black jacket, a tight purple T-shirt. He is frowning at the phone in his hands, walking briskly in the spring afternoon sun. They look across the street at him, enjoying catching this glimpse of him, unguarded.

Hello, they say across the quiet street.

He looks up and a smile transforms him. It is broad and emanates from his entire body. Now his walk is smiling. Instantly light, a bounce in the very next step.

I was not expecting to see you here, he says, beaming.

I know, they say.

They can feel his anticipation and hope as he falls in step with them, the lightness that their presence brings him. His relief that it has begun.

They walk for several hours in Tilburg. Seasonal tries not to smoke too much. They both need a long conversation, to settle into the agreement, to feel more comfortable with each other. During one of the many comfortable silences between them, Seasonal wonders how they will get this tall man onto a beam and if they should have brought their black high heels to give them some extra height and leverage. They have never stood before a restrained person before. Their head spins.

Eventually they return to the house and find their way to each other.

They lie naked together on the couch. László has two, or maybe three, fingers inside Seasonal. He looks into their eyes and asks:

There seems to be an implicit agreement between us, but I want to check. It seems that we are both comfortable with my dick not being involved in what we do.

Seasonal is pleased that he has noticed that they do not touch his dick. He has only used his dick to enter them once or twice, briefly, uneventfully, a kind of tentative, insecure proposition that neither of them have been interested in, so far.

Seasonal struggles their way back from where his touch has taken them. They look in his eyes and arrogantly speak the truth: *I want everything.* But they are also not interested in his pleasure, and so they do not touch his dick—even though they suspect the orgasm they could achieve with it would be spectacular. Somewhere in the back of their mind, low, near the base of their neck, where the central nervous system meets the brain stem, they know that if they can keep him, keep training him, together they will find a way for him to use his dick which is unlike any sex he has ever had.

In the beginning I could not fuck you because I cannot fuck a stranger. And now that I want to fuck you, I find it more interesting not to, he says as he returns his hands between their legs.

I have to tell you that the fact that you do not touch my dick drives me insane, causes me sleepless nights. When I want your touch and you deny me, I think: I hate you, he whispers in their ear.

Seasonal's cunt floods. They casually put their clothes back on and go outside to the small courtyard for a cigarette.

Are you not worried, he asks nonchalantly when they return, *that my frustration will overcome me and I will force myself on you?*

Seasonal looks at him quizzically. He is snacking on precut squares of Gouda from a plastic container.

There is a word in Hungarian for this: fuckrage.

They almost ask him to say the word in Hungarian, and they want to ask about how gender works in Hungarian, but instead they simply say:

No. I am not worried.

With a boyish smile he replies, *Are you not afraid I will not be able to control myself?*

They look at him blankly. *You don't scare me* is the flat response. It is true.

It is not intended as a threat, he says compassionately.

If it was, you are doing a terrible job at it. Casually eating cheese does not really create fear.

How do you imagine you will get to the beam? they ask, redirecting the conversation toward forms of violence less familiar, the forms that have brought them here.

He puts the cheese down and turns his body to face them. *I don't know. I was hoping you could lead me there.*

I can. I will.

László takes the coils of rope that Seasonal had placed on a chair and walks underneath the beam. He quickly has the rope doubled over, the ends aligned and held loosely in his hand. He assesses the height of the beam against his own height—raising his arms, standing on his toes. He reaches to his full height in his tight purple T-shirt and black pants and tries to throw the doubled rope over the beam. His T-shirt rides up to reveal his stomach, the line of hair running from his belly button to his groin. It takes him three tries to throw the rope over the beam. He makes each in quick succession. He is focused, calm, quiet.

Something happens to you when you handle rope. The observation escapes Seasonal's mouth.

It does? He is genuinely surprised.

Yes. Has no one told you before? Has no one described it for you?

No.

I have tried to write it.

He smiles and returns to the task, making two tightly drawn knots, then a small loop where the cuffs can be attached by their clasps.

They find themselves on the couch again. The rope hangs expectantly from the beam a few yards away.

I want to fuck you, he whispers. *I want to come all over your body.*

You don't get to fuck me, Seasonal says matter-of-factly.

They remove his pants and reach for the cuffs.

Quickly and efficiently they guide László into position. He is naked and hanging by his wrists from the rope. They stand and look at him, giving him a few minutes to adjust himself to his new position. Then they ask him how he feels.

It seems a bit late to be saying this, he says meekly, *but I am wondering if I can trust you.*

What can I do to show you you can trust me? they ask benevolently.

He asks them, very sweetly, to take his sex in their mouth.

Yes, they say, running their hands over his smooth torso. *That would be the perfect way to show you you can trust me.*

Instead, they squeeze his testicles hard and long.

He moans in pain. *Please stop* comes low and deep from within him, between the labored deep breaths that sustain him. The reflex in Seasonal's hand fires like a spring. They know they should not stop, but they could not not.

They step back and observe him.

The long ends of the rope fall over his shoulder and run down his torso. His shoulders pulled high by the cuffs, straining against his wrists and the rope. His breathing comes hard and shallow—it is loud, but not musical like his sleeping breathing. He cannot look at them. His eyes are closed. When they stand behind him, the long line of his body is lyric. They want to walk back and take the scene in, but they feel compelled to stay close. To hold him on the rope with their naked body, their presence, their touch, their mouth, their power. When they stand behind him, they sense he feels alone. Maybe next time they will let him feel that loneliness, descend into it. But this first time they want him to know they are here with him. He knows they are here when the pain comes. The longer he hangs, the further he recedes. This is a new side to him. Base. Inward. Breath and slow movement, low sounds of pleasure, of pain, of need, of shame.

When he comes down from the beam, László stands like a new foal. Then he smiles. He leads them to the couch, takes the dildo from the chair.

May I? he says.

He inserts the female end into their slick cunt. The bulbous end fills them but does not reach the depth of Seasonal's desire. He straddles them and lowers himself onto their cock. He is proud of the slut that he is. Getting what he wants, after he has made his offering.

Later, lying in their arms, he thanks them for the pain. He tells them he says *Please stop* because the pain is unbearable and he wants it to stop. But he does not want them to stop. If he really wanted it to end, he would have started counting. This was him begging. This is all he can beg for: cessation.

They next morning, standing in the small courtyard smoking while László eats a breakfast of supermarket bread and hummus, Seasonal admits to their shame about the form and force of their desire.

Why, he says, *because you are not spending your money on a Bakfiets and filling it with three children, but are thinking of installing a hook in your apartment to hang me from instead?* He thinks he is being amusing.

They explain they are well past the shame of not conforming to the normative gendered narrative. It is the object and velocity of their desire that shames them.

When the composer had gotten excited the week before about collaborating with Seasonal on a text-sound work, he said, *This is the future I imagine for you, not one in which you are at home with children and a vacuum cleaner.* Seasonal finds both men's way of speaking to the woman in them clumsy.

László does not understand their shame. His own shame is obvious to him, Seasonal's is not. *This is gendered,* they think. The desire for domination is obvious and not shameful to the masculine point of view. Seasonal tries again to explain their predicament:

The objects of our play are all with me. These objects you make me carry, they say things, they speak. You leave it all with me. You can walk away as though none of this happened. I carry them. They sit in my house. They speak when I do not want them to, they say things—they say things I am not always wanting to hear. If people see them, they speak to them too. I cannot stop them.

László looks at them blankly. Seasonal disappears into their own shame, their own dim questions. He disappears.

After they return home, Seasonal goes onto the internet to try to find *fuckrage* in Hungarian. But their ability to search the Hungarian version of the internet is nonexistent. After a few days of fruitless trying, they relent and admit they are a stranger. The ask for László's help:

> *how does one*
> *say "fuckrage" in*
> *Hungarian?*

The answer comes immediately:

Baszdüh

Seasonal notices the word shares in his *sz*.

I Am My Own Restraints

I thought my goal
was to hang on
a beam and I
needed to find the
right person who
could facilitate that.

I learned that
it is the other
way around.

What I need is
a person I can
trust and whose
desires complement
mine, and the

beam is just one way to find that person and find that trust.

I had a dream
last night

I was in your
house, or rather,
somewhere together

I don't know
exactly where

I was blind and
deaf

My ears, eyes,
mouth covered
tightly

With tape or
a hood, I don't
know

It deprived me
of time and space
and locked me
inside, and at the
same time locked
me out from
myself

All the world
had become was
your presence

Hinted by the
feeling of the
stirring of the
air as you passed
my chained and
naked and hanging
body

By the occasional
touch,

By the pain that
came with
unpredictable force
and frequency

The feeling that I
am no more than
any other object
in the room with
the single function
to serve your
comfort

Humiliated me,
made me hard and
wet.

Each time I sensed
your proximity, I
was hoping you'd
touch my sex,
give me pleasure,
comfort, release

But instead it
was your pleasure,
it was your comfort,
your release when
you fucked me
and ignored me.
When you used
my body to
learn to hurt.

And this left me
dripping, half-mad
from denial, and
confused, but
ultimately happy
as I never was
before.

what was it like
to wake up from
this dream?

I did not wake up
from this dream

My skin is the
only sense I have

One raw surface
my body is.

I had a fantasy
this morning, still
half-asleep in my
bed.

I was standing
in your living room,
chained naked to
the wall by my
neck.

While you had a
party, with guests
walking talking
having wine.

This time there
was no hood, no
blindfold, nothing
to hide behind
from the people,
from your friends.

I remember the
feeling of not
knowing whether to
avert my eyes
from those looking at
me, or meet their
gazes with shame

(275)

and pride.

tell me more
about this feeling?

This feeling is the
feeling I learn to
recognize and feel
in our exchange.

The feeling of
embracing my very
private feelings in public

Liberating and
horrifying

I am my own
restraints.

When you make me
beg, when I'm
bound and at
your mercy, my
restraints do not
matter anymore.

Seasonal's father was a carpenter for most of their childhood. When Seasonal was twelve years old, he fell from the roof of a house he was building and smashed his leg. This accident allowed him to return to his first love: computers. Over the nearly twenty years that he was building houses, he imparted to his sons a lot of knowledge of construction. Seasonal can identify just about all the tools a carpenter uses. As a child she accompanied her father to worksites and it was her job to bring him the tools he needed from his van. It never occurred to her father that Seasonal would have liked to know how to use the tools she was taught to fetch. She can't remember when she realized he was not going to teach her.

After the night on the beam in Tilburg and the dreaming, László and Seasonal are keen to meet again. They make arrangements.

I would like to have
at least twenty-four
hours in your presence.

In anticipation and disbelief, Seasonal opens the web browser on their computer and tries to learn the Dutch names of the tools and materials they will need to restrain László in their apartment. They make an online order from the consumer hardware store Gamma:

- 1 × Black+Decker accuschroefklopboormachine BDCHD18KB-QW 18 volt
- 1 × Ketting gesmeed korte schakel A-40 3 meter
- 2 × Aanlegring thermisch verzinkt 55 × 55 mm

- 2 × Karabijnhaak verzinkt 60 mm
- 1 × GAMMA schroef universeel assortiment platkop verzinkt 550 stuks

A drill. Tethers. Three yards of chain that can hold up to one hundred and eighty pounds. Clips to attach the chain to the tethers. Screws.

Over the coming days, while moving around their apartment in the service of everyday life, they pause to envision László's vertical naked body in different spaces. In doorways, in corners, on the landing. Eventually, they decide that the best place for him to be suspended is between the two large cupboards that hold most of their books: philosophy, cultural criticism, gender theory, and literature. They do not like to have their library on display. The white cupboards are stuffed with books, kept in idiosyncratic order. The left cupboard holds scholarly works. The right cupboard holds literature, nonfiction, comics. The cupboards frame the sliding doors that separate the living room from the dining room. He can be suspended on this threshold, between the wings of their library.

Before the package from the hardware store can arrive, Seasonal travels by train to Paris to see a very dear friend play a concert of experimental music that will be broadcast on French public radio. They attend the performance in the Radio France Auditorium, a big round building on the banks of the Seine built in 2014, but which feels like it was built in the 1970s. It is located in the unfashionable, upmarket sixteenth arrondissement—the home of bankers, corporate functionaries, and retired executives. The concert is arranged by an important French collective in the field of electroacoustic music that is renowned for its speaker array. Forty-eight speakers are set up in the auditorium, including two speaker trees that sit in the audience. *They are only for treble*, their friend later explains. The boughs of the speaker trees remind Seasonal of Dr. Seuss: quirky angels and curves. The speakers are design objects, mostly in white and concrete grey. Eight bright-red round speakers, each on one leg, form a wide semicircle across the stage like a chorus line. Two large grey speakers, echoing the posture of industrial fans, sit further back. And then there are the less showy familiar black speakers, collected together in neat rectangles suspended from the ceiling at a precise angle. When each of the four pieces in the evening's program is performed, subtle theatre lighting picks out a group of speakers from the dark. The performer, their equipment and instrument, and the speakers are illuminated with pillows of light, emulating the dawn.

Of the four pieces commissioned for the concert, three of them involve acoustic instruments being put in relation to digital technology—the laptop on stage, alongside a Steinway, then a trumpet, a cello. None of these musician-composers seem to have any love for their instrument. The musicians do not want the instruments to make the sounds they have been crafted to make, and which the musicians have no doubt trained for years to learn how to coax from the wood, the strings, the metal using their breath, their fingers, their muscles, their brains, their personalities, their souls. They work the acoustic instruments against themselves—reaching into the Steinway to place objects on its strings, bashing the keys with their elbows so fast their arms are a blur, live sampling and looping the trumpet until it sounds like a raving lunatic. Seasonal watches and listens in awe and confusion. This is a different kind of torture. It is not dominance, like in the frescoes of Florence and in the Rijksmuseum. This is aggression made of dedication. Seasonal wonders: *Is the audience here for fuckrage?*

In sharp contrast to their interactions with the instruments, the musicians touch the dials of their samplers and the keyboards of their laptop computers with the loving, delicate gesture of a mother removing an eyelash from the cheek of her sleeping infant.

Seasonal's friend is the only one who has composed a work that involves an analog machine. His piece is written for computer and Hammond organ and its spinning Leslie speaker. Like the other performers, he has a laptop on stage, but he only attends to it at the beginning of the piece and then gives all his attention to the organ. Seasonal has no idea what role the laptop plays in what ensues. The Hammond organ is a demanding instrument, with peddles and switches as well as the keys to operate. They have known their friend since he was eighteen years old, and they can see how every fiber of his being is focused on the complex set of movements and timings required to make the organ sound as good as it can. Later he will say to them:

I just wanted to make some really great organ music, you know?

He rocks back and forth to the private rhythm of his music and he appears to Seasonal—who has not spent much time listening to or thinking about experimental electroacoustic music and is clearly biased because of the love they have for him—to be the only one of the performers who wants the music he is making, who is not using the performance as a vehicle for something he cannot face.

After the performance, the two of them sit outside a café in the quiet, unfashionable suburb. The spring evening is languid and inviting, punctuated occasionally by the sharp, frantic sound of a scooter. Seasonal has one cigarette left in their pack, and they are avoiding smoking it. They ask their friend how things are going now that he has recommitted to his twenty-year marriage, after a tumultuous eighteen months.

I think it is the hardest thing I have ever done, he replies as a scooter roars past. Seasonal mishears him and walks away thinking he has said *bravest*.

The next day, with the misheard word in their ears, Seasonal is on the Paris subway, traveling back to the hotel after a visit to the Palais de Tokyo. Their phone draws their attention away from the people in the subway car. László wants to talk about books.

O *is the most*
exciting

I can identify with
the heroine :)

please give me a
description of this
identification ... ?

I have a deep-
seated desire that
someone takes me
through that journey
O went through

have you asked
anyone to do that?

or do you enjoy
it as a fantasy?

No I haven't found
anyone I trusted
enough to ask such
a thing. You are
the first person I
trust enough for
such a request.

...

What is your take
on O?

Having never read *The Story of O* because of their disinterest in female submission, Seasonal lies.

> *i need to*
> *reread it.*
>
> *i would like to*
> *read it through*
> *you.*

:)

> *:)*

I wonder if you'd
be up for such
a voyage

It is almost 1:00 a.m. Seasonal lies in their tiny hotel room. They read his last message as a disrespectful dare, and they would like to slap his face.

> *i would like you*
> *to say what you*
> *want from o's*
> *voyage.*
>
> *which parts.*
> *which features.*
> *which experiences.*

*I need to reread
it, but the first
part of the book
when O is taken
by the hand by
her lover and going
through her training
was very very
appealing.*

> *i am trying to
> get you to say
> it :) rather
> than let o speak
> for you. and i
> like how elegantly
> you go around
> this invitation.
> but i also remain
> steadfast in my
> desire for you
> to give your
> own form to your
> desire to be taken
> by the hand and
> trained.*

*I would like to
ask you this
question again when*

we are in the
same room. I want
to say it to
you, beg you, ask
you, instead of
writing it down
on this soulless
surface of ephemera.

:)

i know you would
prefer this. but i
have been using you,
and our interactions
in this medium,
from the beginning.
keeping you writing
here is a fundamental
drive of mine,
and i won't give up
pursuing it while
it captivates and
inspires me.

László sends the black heart emoji.

You taught me
something again,
thank you.

                                        :) what was it?

Forms of engagement,
that I once
knew but forgot

I started to write:
train me

But I hesitated.
Train me in what?

O was trained in
obedience and in
the acceptance of
being used by
random men

But I'm not sure
if this is the thing
you want to engrain
in me

                                        what are the forms
                                        of engagement you
                                                forgot?

(286)

Spontaneous, open,
carefree, inspiring
:)

                                                    :)

Relaxed.

                                        i understand
                                what you just learned.
                                        and i am so
                                    pleased you have
                                    been reminded of
                                    the other meanings
                                        of play :)

The next morning, Seasonal buys a copy of *The Story of O* in the Abbey Bookshop in Paris and rides the Thalys back to the Netherlands. In the Dutch style, their downstairs neighbor had accepted the package from the hardware store when the delivery driver arrived earlier that day. Seasonal knocks on the door in the evening. The heavily pregnant *buurvrouw* opens the door, her eighteen-month-old son on her hip. They greet each other briefly, and Seasonal picks up the package from the hallway floor. The boy has just woken up from his afternoon nap. They coax a smile out of him and he turns shyly into his mother's brown hair.

They next morning, directly above the growing family's living and dining room, Seasonal begins the process of installing the two tethers into the door frame. They send messages to Y, who has twenty-five years' experience in handling tools and working with materials. They consult her on the placement of the tethers. They assemble their drill and discover the hardwood frame will not yield to the self-tapping screws. They take the short walk to their local hardware store and buy a set of drill bits. Seasonal had hoped to be able to undertake this transaction in Dutch, but the woman in the hardware store quickly exceeds their rudimentary vocabulary. They switch to English and soon they are walking back to their apartment with the drill bits in the pockets of their black cotton jacket, alongside a new container of water-based personal lubricant from the shop across the street from the hardware store.

They stand on their dining room table and the hardwood takes the 3 mm drill bit easily. The smell of wood yielding to spinning steel reminds them of their childhood—the squeal of the circular saw coming from the backyard as their father cut timber for frames for houses. With relative speed and efficiency, Seasonal has the two tethers in place. This activity feels familiar from their theatre-making youth. They are constructing a set.

They sit and drink tea and admire their handiwork, and then they go to bed. As they fall asleep they wonder, *Why am I not dreaming?* László's reports of his dreams are vivid and powerful, yet Seasonal's sleep is long and imageless. They wake feeling peaceful and rested.

Later that morning, a heavy spring shower wets the neighborhood, and a message arrives from László, announcing he is en route.

I am too clean

> *why do you*
> *feel too clean?*

I had a bath this
morning, which is
always a sort of
ritual cleansing before
our meetings. But
I lost my smells,
my grit in the
process this time.

> *a clean slate :)*

I hope there
wasn't too much
washed off

When he arrives, László does indeed look clean and neatly dressed. Seasonal welcomes him into the living room, and he removes a ring from his middle finger and places it on the white mantlepiece. He goes to the toilet, and Seasonal inspects the ring: it is made of two curved pieces of interlocked metal. Rust and silver, well-worn. Seasonal has seen it before, at an earlier meeting, and when they asked him about it he explained that he liked to work with silver and materials that are fragile, decaying. He liked to see how long things could stay together, and to watch them come apart.

May I come closer? he asks upon returning to the room.

Yes.

May I kiss you?

No.

They stand close together, looking, smelling, sensing.

Seasonal invites him upstairs, to climb out the window to the inaccessible balcony outside their bedroom. They stand together overlooking the gardens that run behind the apartment building, a secluded bricked-in space. Two floors below, the downstairs neighbors are *samenwerking* with the next-door neighbors to remove the established Italian jasmine that grows atop their adjacent garden sheds. The roof needs replacing, so the jasmine must go. The friendly round vowels of Dutch small talk waft upward on the fragrant spring air. Above them, László stands tall and diffident and full of longing.

May I kiss you? he asks.

No. I think you should climb back through the window and take all your clothes off, Seasonal says calmly.

He obeys. A grateful, expectant look settles on his face as he removes his black pants, his black T-shirt. Standing in his underwear, he raises his eyebrows.

These too?

He lies naked on the bed. Seasonal kisses his mouth slowly, then traces a line with their tongue down his neck to his shoulder. He sighs. They sense his body slackening. They kiss him again, and then place two fingers in their mouth and run their fingers across the plump flesh of his anus. He sighs again, they feel his sphincter muscles twitch and soften beneath the gentle pressure of their fingers. They let him welcome them.

The first time I allowed myself to follow my desire for men, I went to a bathhouse. I had to shut off everything to go there, to be there, and they could see it, that I had no defenses. Before I knew it I was surrounded and I could feel hands on my body, a finger in my ass.

Seasonal's finger moves slowly inside László as he tells this story. This part of him is soft and thick and pillowy. The softness reaches his eyes when he cannot hide his need to let go, to be taken over. They would like to disappear into this part of him, to fill him entirely. He is open and firm. As he talks, the air in the bedroom thickens with his shame. They push their finger deeper, he gives his shame form in a low, deep moan. His pride, the muddy green of his eyes, his long limbs—a lure. They wonder if any of the men in that bathhouse saw what they see so clearly: the sharply delineated figure wrapped in the confident outer shell. The figure inside wants to surrender, to be led, to be taken and possessed. The figure uses those muddy-green eyes to signal a gaping hole wanting to be filled.

The way you put your finger in my ass just now makes me think you know how to touch a woman, he says softly, his long arm draped across their back.

You are the best girl I know, they instinctively respond. The smile lights his eyes.

Seasonal cannot stop the smile coming to their face in response. It is true. The way he loves to be fucked. They recognize that eagerness. It is theirs. On their hands and knees. Face in the sheets. Overcome with the need to be filled, to receive someone else's power, to feel like the ant under the precisely angled magnifying glass, bursting into flames. The soft gratefulness. The feeling of having been given a unique gift. Of being so lucky. It is as close to their own annihilation as they can bear to come.

The arrogance of their dom self is punctured, briefly, by the sense of how they are refracting in, through, by, with László. A new set of capacities which they had only dimly sensed is now coursing in their muscles, their cunt, their blood, their mind. The possibility throngs. They know nothing about gender, as they have lived it, as it has demanded that they live. They feel ashamed of the power they have given it, of the attention it has taken. Its grip on their desire, their comportment, their speech, their writing, their life force cannot hold now that they are entangled with László's submission. This is not the shedding of a skin, or the malting of a winter coat, the losing of baby teeth, or even the emergence from a cocoon. It is a walk outside the walls of the Republic, without having been anointed or thanked.

But László wants to thank them, for placing their fingers gently inside him and hearing his story of the bathhouse. For dissolving the shame in pleasure. He lays Seasonal on their back. He kneels between their legs. They stretch out, enjoying their length, enjoying the view of him there between their legs. He looks up the length of their slim torso to their eyes. He looks serious, focused. His hands disappear. They close their eyes. His fingers become a force. They do not feel the vast emptiness they have always associated with wanting to be touched, to be penetrated, to be filled. Instead, they feel a strong sense of completeness, of openness, of unashamed curiosity and pleasure. They open their eyes and seek his gaze. They feel him working his way through their openness. Their eyes are locked. His touch reaches into their body with all the power of the pride he feels in his submission. It has something of his arrogance too. Of the face he shows the world, of the straight posture and charisma they've seen the echoes of when they met him after he left the meeting in Brussels. It has a trace of his leadership in it. But it is deeply humble, stripped of its context and purpose. He delivers his power to them to thank them for fucking him like a slut. For not caring about his pleasure. For not touching his dick, and for not letting him come the way he knows how to come. He converts his power into service, and with half his hand inside them he twists his wrist and pushes deeper. They register a new cadence of pleasure—of being taken apart whilst being entirely rooted in their wholeness.

Afterward, they are hungry and agree to go out for a bite before exploring the question of László on the tethers Seasonal has installed. Before they leave the house to find food, Seasonal shows László the tethers. He radiates gratitude.

You do not submit in the abstract, he says as they eat their pasta, *you submit to the person. I know that now. You have taught me that.*

Seasonal's smile is wide and bright. They look around the tidy urban streetscape, at the cyclists, the parents walking with their children to get ice cream, the light posts with their tubs of red geraniums. Nothing in this late-spring setting confirms to them that they have achieved their goal, that with these words László announces that they are entering a new level of the collaboration where, perhaps, finally, they can begin to be the one who learns.

They take a short walk after eating and return to the apartment. The light in the sky has faded by the time László asks for a third time to be attached to the tethers. Once he is there, his wrists clipped to the tether points by the cuffs, his vulnerability is radiant. Seasonal takes his testicles in the palm of their hand. The deep intake of his breath marks the beginning. They bite his nipple, they squeeze his balls, they take his tongue in their mouth. He is less panicked than the first time he was suspended, in Tilburg. The trust he has in them cushions his fear now. They have less fear too. Less shame. They use their teeth with blunt intention on his flesh. They create waves of pain in which he can be lost: tightening and releasing their hand and teeth. Their desire to own him, the impossibility of this desire, the paradox of their will to annihilate him in order to celebrate his existence and autonomy, produces an intense incomprehension. They take the compressed force of this intolerable need—hard like steel—and write with it on his body.

No no no no no no no no no no no.
Please. No.
No no no no no no.

Useless refusals rush from his mouth, the sound absorbed by the thick rug beneath his feet. There is no power behind the short sounds, they are meek and quiet and pleading. Ephemeral. The *no* Seasonal has been pursuing arrives and proliferates in a pattern and form they could not have predicted. Their clitoris swells. Their ruthlessness rises. The *noes* bounce like hail stones and they maintain their grip on his body and will.

Seasonal orchestrates an increase in the pain on his scrotum and László disappears. He leaves his eyes, present only in shallow breath. They maintain the pressure to hold him there. They release their hand after what could be a few more seconds or minutes and kiss his neck, breathe in his heavy smell. They look at his face. He is far away, head limp on his neck. They rest their forearm across his chest, their hand in his armpit, feeling the dampness there. They hold him with the low, steady energy of their strength and attention. A smile appears. He returns to his eyes.

There you are, they whisper.

He smiles and nods.

Reclining on their couch afterward, László asks to be taken there again, for longer. Past himself. He wants Seasonal to lead him there, to be there with him. He can only go there knowing they will be his companion on the journey.

I know it is a lot to ask, he says with strong eye contact, curled under the orange, purple, blue, and red squares of the blanket Seasonal brought with them from their grandmother's house in Australia. The absolute certainty of his desire, and the fragility of his need, gives his look a compelling clarity.

Yes. Absolutely.

But as Seasonal says this they are also wondering about what one can ask for. If you say *Hello, World?* and the world says *Hello* back, then what?

The next morning, László showers and prepares to leave. Seasonal watches it. Greedily. With the alchemical mix of feelings that periodically overwhelmed them in their childhood—hope, thirsty need, a vast sense of being undeserving, of not being the kind of person the wished-for thing would choose.

He says *Goodbye* at the top of the stairs. His eyes gentle, recalling the deep channel of his submission.

They lock the door behind him and return to the first floor.

It is still there.

They wait an hour or so. Then they snap a photo of the ring with their phone and send it to him.

Objects, objects,
betraying me

This was not
intentional

Objects on the Path
to Annihilation

The rust-and-silver ring finds its home in the small metal box their mother gave Seasonal for Christmas when they were visiting Australia. Its only companion is a single type block for letterpress, a comma/apostrophe, bought at the Clignancourt flea market in Paris years ago. Before putting the ring in the box, Seasonal cannot resist slipping it on the finger they had inside László when he bared his shame, when he asked them not to use their finger because it brought back the bathhouse. The finger they pushed deeper inside him to push the shame out. The middle finger of their left hand.

The ring slides over their wide knuckle easily. It sits loose, but secure, on the long lower portion of their finger. Its effect is instantaneous. The new alchemical mix of feelings overcomes them: rage, desire, omnipotence, benevolence, the will to power, the full force of their will to master. Their skin electrifies. They feel every one of their ribs. Their cunt is a deep well of knowledge. Seasonal marvels at the ring.

The deep brown of the rust is not as companionable with their skin tone as it is with László's. But of all the objects he has brought as offerings, left behind, pretended to forget, and lost, this one unleashes something they thought only his body could. Underneath the potency of dominance comes the sharp, acid sting of humiliation. At coveting the object. At the deep, affirming pleasure training him, hurting him, denying him, knowing better than him brings them. The ring pushes their pleasure and shame to the surface. They stand alone in their bedroom, transfixed, lost, charged, fragile, and aching.

The ring ignites a new desire: Seasonal wants something to use on László's body that magnetizes them like the rust-and-silver ring. Another prosthetic like the dildo that will amplify László's need to submit. They know László likes the threat of pain almost as much as he likes the pain itself. A few days after he left the ring behind, they ask a question:

> *are there objects that*
> *attract, compel, or*
> *interest you?*

yes. and no.
yes, because i am
interested in how
objects i like
interact with my
senses.

No, because if an
object's sole capacity,

*role, or raison
d'etre is to
deliver pain, I'm
not interested*

*I'm more curious
about repurposing
objects for the
delivery of pain
than visiting the
torture museum. :)*

*:)
so i would like
to give you a
task.*

*do you want
one?*

yes!

*i want you to
find and repurpose
an object and
bring it to me to
use on your
restrained body.*

will you do
that for me?

Yes.

Seasonal beams with satisfaction that the simple answers come from him without struggle. They wonder what challenges making the object will bring him. In a few days, this question is answered:

I would like to
ask about the task
you've given me.

I think I did
the more difficult
one of the two
ideas I had
in mind.

But I started to
have doubts if I
understood the task
correctly.

In addition, I'm
trying to understand
my role in finding
this object.

I also remember
what you had said
about the bamboo
stick you had in
mind,

that you know
where to find it,
and you know
that this is
what you want.

I am very happy
to bring you
objects I find
relevant in relation
to pain.

But my ultimate
desire is to submit
myself to the pain
you give the way
that fulfils your desire.

i know it is

the tension you
feel has a purpose

the choice between
your own desire
and mine

decentering you means
creating situations where
you might have to
choose between pursuing
your desire, and
pursuing your
submission and its
pleasures

You taught me not
to be ashamed
of my desires, and
to bring them to
you with joy
and pride.

I think now
that I was searching
for a solution in
the wrong place.

I wanted to find
an object that I was
hoping would please
you.

*Now I understand
that I need to find
an object which
would please me.*

Is that correct?

Seasonal was trying to be a good student. While their body was leading, their brain didn't want to be left out. Over the last few months, they had been reading all the classics of literature and philosophy on sadism and masochism. *Venus in Furs* and the philosopher Gilles Deleuze's accompanying essay, the Marquis de Sade, Charlotte Brontë's *Villette*, *The Story of O.* Years ago, while living in the Riverina in Australia, home of the Wiradjuri—the hot, dry agricultural region through which the great Murray-Darling river system flows—Seasonal had attended a book sale at the Wagga Wagga City Library on a sunny Saturday morning with H. Amongst the pile of hundreds of deaccessioned works of literature and philosophy they browsed, Seasonal had picked up the hardcover copy of Simone de Beauvoir's essay *Must We Burn Sade?* As a good feminist, they knew they had to take Beauvoir home. They had felt sad looking at all the books the library no longer had a use for, but they were also surprised that anyone had thought that people farming out here would want to read Beckett or Beauvoir at the end of a long day. Walking away with H and their pile of books toward the farmer's market, they wondered about the librarian who had thought, *Oh yes, we should have Beauvoir's book on Sade.* Vertically written on the title page was the information: *Book Supplies 30.01.74, $3.96.* Seasonal had added the book to their library when they got home and not read it. Like many of the books they bought, they wanted it for the potential it signified. Years later, much closer to Beauvoir's home and much farther from their own, Seasonal was finally reading it and underlining passages. This morning, it was this passage that had grabbed their attention:

The world of the masochist is a magical one, and that is why he is almost always a fetishist. Objects, such as shoes, furs, and whips, are charged with emanations which have the power to change him into a thing, and that is precisely what he wants, to remove himself by becoming an inert object.

Hours later, Seasonal walks their friend's Dutch sheepdog along the Amstel River. It is an evening in the early summer, C and her son are away and Seasonal is dog-sitting. The wide surface of the river is busy with water birds, people in kayaks, teams of amateur rowers, and groups of young men in pleasure boats blasting music made with the heavy use of autotune. They admire the simple leather collar on the dog as she walks with them.

In two weeks from now, Seasonal will catch a train to Berlin, where László is spending two months working on his book on the internet. They will spend a week with him there. They don't really know why they are going. All they know is that they cannot not go.

In the golden light along the river, they are wondering what freedom László seeks in his submission. *I am my own restraints*, he had said. He has told Seasonal he wants freedom from the authority of his ego: he is trying to find a way to walk away from the reality it creates, the way he walked away from Hungary as a community of fate. László sees himself as a freedom fighter, fighting hardest of all, perhaps, for his own sense of peace and space and joy and security. As the rowers glide by, Seasonal realizes they spend too much time thinking about László … What is it that they are seeking?

Their mind bucks this question. It is easier to think about László, to train their mind on him and satisfy their will to master, than to ponder the murky, wide waters of their own desire and fear. They force their mind to their own position—*Forget him*, they say in the voice of their superego. *What are you seeking?*

Joggers pound the asphalt beside them. Their walking pace is steady and brisk. It belies their certainty. Their mind is no help, so they ask their body. They ask their cells, which excite at the thought of more than twenty-four hours of him. They ask the palm of their hand, which remembers the force it brought to the softest parts of his body. They ask their cervix, which he touched last time they met. They ask their anus, which told them to beg for a third finger from him. They ask their ear canal, which caught the whisper *I remember that sound* and the echo of his orgasm over the data connection from South Korea. Their body feels the strong, deep current of their attraction to his submission, to the forms it takes and has not yet taken. But they do not know why they flow this way, slowly toward something that is not him per se, but is the scene of his annihilation.

Their cells, their hands, their cunt, their ass, their skin, their ears— they all give the same answer: *annihilation*. The word has a thickness. They cannot say it aloud. It is the only word they have for their desire, and so it is a private word. They pause and sit on the bench by the river, hearing the answer from their body, the word lying on their tongue. Where the tip of their tongue rests lightly against the roof of their mouth, they feel *annihilation* take its place. Like salt flakes. Thin. Sharp. Unmistakable. Almost too much.

They sit beside the river in order to swallow the salty lust of annihilation. The dog looks at them quizzically, her mouth open in a smile. She accepts the pause in the walk and begins to explore the tall grass and cigarette butts around the bench. She chews some grass. She gets to know the ground through her nose.

Seasonal looks up the definition of *annihilation* on their phone. *The Encyclopedia Britannica* website tells them:

Annihilation, in physics, a reaction in which a particle and its antiparticle collide and disappear, releasing energy. The most common annihilation on Earth occurs between an electron and its antiparticle, a positron. A positron … usually combines briefly with an electron to form a quasi-atom called positronium. The quasi-atom is composed of the two particles spinning around each other before they annihilate. After the annihilation, two or three gamma rays radiate from the point of collision.

Seasonal walks back along the river with the dog, enters the apartment, feeds the dog, and cooks and eats dinner, lost in a feeling question about annihilation.

While they have been doing this, László has also been trying to find the words for a feeling.

Berlin for me is
about having the
time and the space
to immerse myself in
your desires, and
mine.

I am prepared to
hand over my
autonomy, and lock
myself up in
your will.

It is harder to
put this into
writing than I
thought.

It feels like I'm
opening up my
body and soul to
accommodate your
body and desire,
to satisfy.

I don't know
what of all the
possibilities will be
the key that
opens the doors
on our boundaries.

But I would like,
at the same time,
to be fucked by
you in public,
and spend the

week bound up
and beaten in
a room.

I want to provoke
you, inspire you,
please you, unsettle
you, be the slut
you can lead
down the road
on a leash.

I will mark both
my tongue and
anus to mark
that they serve you.

I would like to
carry your marks
on my body
after you leave.

Lying in bed, reading these messages, Seasonal is afraid, again, that there is not enough time. They came to László to try to understand the dark place in themself: the abyss of fear and subjection that was installed in them by the atmosphere of threat and violence and shouting that is all they really remember of their childhood. They want to build a scale model of control, tyranny, violence, subjection, and total power. They are trying to build it with consent, with care, with ethics. They want to write this scene with their body, and make it anew each time they write it. They want to build the model so they can understand how it worked. They want to know each and every part of the structure of subjugation. Each beam and stud the carpenter used in the frame. Each entry and exit point for the electricity, the water, the gas. How the air flows in and out of the domestic interior that is the space of intimate tyranny. They want to find a way out of this system of domination, to walk away from the scene that shaped them the way László walked away from Hungary. They are hoping this new object that he is making will become a tool to help them in this study.

In the morning, a message arrives.

I'm formulating a letter
to you that I'd
like to give you
in person if that
is OK with you.

A few days later, their dog-sitting duties completed, Seasonal goes home and tries to sit in the sun as often as it shows its face in the rainy Dutch summer.

The night before they each leave the Netherlands for Berlin, László and Seasonal are chatting while they pack.

half my bag is
taken up with objects
to fuck & restrain
you … what are
you packing? ;)

Books.

Seasonal is also packing books. There is not a lot of room in their duffle bag, once they pack an extra pair of black jeans, ten black T-shirts, chain, the cuffs, two dildos, a roll of gaffer tape, lubricant, three pieces of rope, their harness, and their laptop. Their small toiletry bag carries the earplugs they use against László's snoring. At the bottom of the bag are the books: the hardcover of Beauvoir's essay on Sade, *The Story of O*, Nin's *Delta of Venus*, and a large collected works of Sade which includes *Justine* and *Philosophy in the Bedroom*.

In their backpack, Seasonal packs *The Sparrow* by Mary Doria Russell. They want to read it on the train to learn more about László's submission. He had mentioned the book when they were walking in Tilburg preparing themselves for him to face the beam. He had presented a long anecdote which required him to summarize the premise of the book. He had just told them he wanted to hang on the beam like a dead body and be used.

A Jesuit priest goes on a mission to an alien planet. He is taken hostage there and used as a sex slave. All kinds of horrible things are done to him. He returns to Earth and he is broken, traumatized. The entire novel tells the story of the community asking him to tell them what happened, and him being unable to.

The community want to know. They want to hear his story so he can heal. But he cannot tell them. He has no words for what was done to him.

Am I the aliens? Seasonal wondered as László talked. They felt dizzy.

Who am I in this analogy? They finally asked with trepidation.

The community, László replied simply. His smile was broad and grateful.

Seasonal could not respond in words, hoping that their treatment of his restrained body showed him that he was not wrong.

As they finish packing their bag, Seasonal is reminded of another story about books László had told. This one was public, and he shared it with them before they had met in person. While they were chatting in the dating app, László had shared a link to a piece of his own writing. It discussed the principles of Open Access publishing and was structured by an autobiographical account of him returning to Budapest with his partner to pack up their shared library of thousands of books.

My tears cut deep grooves into the dust on my face. Drip, drip, drop, they hit the floor and disappear among the torn pages scattered on the floor.

This year it dawned on us that we cannot postpone it any longer: our personal library has to go. Our family moved countries more than half a decade ago, we switched cultures, languages, and chose another future. But the past, in the form of a few thousand books in our personal library, was still neatly stacked in our old apartment, patiently waiting, books that we bought and enjoyed—and forgot; books that we bought and never opened; books that we inherited from long-dead parents and half-forgotten friends. Some of them were important. Others were relevant at one point but no longer, yet they still reminded us who we once were.

When we moved, we took no more than two suitcases of personal belongings. The books were left behind. The library was like a sick child or an ailing parent, it hung over our heads like an unspoken threat, a curse. It was clear that sooner or later something had to be done about it, but none of the options available offered any consolation. It made no sense to move three thousand books to the other side of this continent. We decided to emigrate, and not to take our past with us, abandon the contexts we were fleeing from. We made a choice to leave behind the history, the discourses, the problems and the pain that accumulated in the books of our library. I knew exactly what it was I didn't want to teach to my children once we moved.

We are killers, gutting our library.

When they read this account almost a year ago, they were surprised by the reversal. The only thing Seasonal had taken from Australia was their library.

Questions of Potency

Seasonal almost misses the train from Amsterdam to Berlin because of Amsterdam Pride. They drag the duffle bag weighed down with books and rope and cuffs across the platform at Utrecht Centraal Station. The platform is groaning under the weight of hundreds of excited people dressed in bright colors trying to board the direct train to Amsterdam Centraal Station.

On the six-hour journey across Germany, Seasonal tries to chat with László via WhatsApp. They get answers to their probing questions but they are only of a word or two and yield no information about the state he is in. They cannot get him on the hook. As the day unfolds on the train, they read Beauvoir on Sade and *The Sparrow* by Mary Doria Russell. They find Russell's rendering of the traumatized protagonist too painful to read and give up after less than hour. Instead they watch Germany out the window and listen to Keith Jarrett's *Köln Concert* on repeat. They snack on nuts and drink black tea from the thermos they filled from the teapot before they left their apartment.

An hour away from Berlin Ostbahnhof, having sat with their uneasiness about arriving with no sense of László, they open their web browser and book a room at the five-star hotel around the corner from the apartment he has rented. They immediately feel relieved. The ball is back in their court, they can lead.

Once at the hotel, they arrange to meet László nearby, and the two of them agree that food is the first priority. Over mediocre mezze, László notices people looking at Seasonal.

Does this happen to you in Amsterdam? In Utrecht? That people look at you? They look, and then they look again.

They had not noticed it today because Seasonal was too busy looking at him. After not seeing him for a month, they are trying to adjust to his presence, and trying not to get run over. They are no longer used to walking in cities with cars.

Yes, it happens all the time. They are probably trying to work out what gender I am, they guess nonchalantly.

He nods. *I guess I thought that in Berlin you could be whoever you are and no one would care …*

Seasonal almost admires his utopian belief that there might be spaces where gender does not exist.

They ask László if he has read *The City & The City* by China Miéville.

Yes. I love it. They smile at each other.

I think queer and straight culture are like the two countries in that novel. They share space and unsee each other. There are plenty of people on the streets here that look like me, but these people unsee them. They are looking at me and are confused because they realize they have looked across the divide.

As they say this, they understand how much they relish this position. That they like sitting across the table from a man whose gender presentation is as clear as László's. They like the oblique angle of light each projects onto the other.

After mezze, they walk for hours in the warm summer evening, following the Spree. At the beginning of the walk László tries to summarize the letter he has written to them and which he left on the table in his apartment.

I want to learn to give back.

They ask László to study them the way they have studied him. If they have any hope of crossing their boundaries, their fear and fascination with giving pain, of taking what they want without asking, of the dependency of dominance upon submission, they need his ingenuity, his attention, his knowledge.

I have to apologize, they say as they are trying to find their way back to the apartment, *sometimes I don't hear what you are saying because my desire is screaming so loudly in my ears.*

A list of things that overwhelm them while walking with László along the Spree in the dark:

- To find a beautiful young man to fuck László while they watch
- To restrain him for an entire day and write him
- To walk into a party with him on a lead, and have everyone in the room know they made him
- To never let anyone know they made him, to deny him the pleasure of the pride in his submission by telling him he can never mention their exchange to anyone
- To put him on a plane and send him to Y as a present

- To make a scar, which runs diagonally from his shoulder to his hip, which disrupts the smooth, flawless open field of his skin, and which is the mark of their possession. For that scar to rise like a mountain range out of the fault lines of the exchange.

Seasonal does not want to enter the apartment. They want to take a shower. They hand him the second key to the hotel room and invite him to visit if he wants to. The ground-floor windows of the hotel are perpetually shattered, in an ongoing protest against the gentrification of Kreuzberg. J and her partner had lived two blocks from here in their final years in Berlin, walking their dog in the morning amongst the punks and queers who were yet to find their way home after a long night of dancing.

When László arrives at their hotel door long after midnight, knocking quietly, he has changed into a black shirt and pants. He is fresh.

I took a shower too, he says quietly, openly.

Seasonal sits on the edge of the bed in their underwear and the silk shirt they have been wearing all day. The one that they button to the neck and which is, apparently, more androgynous than they thought. When they selected it to wear to their job interview at the Dutch university, they thought this large, black shirt was almost a move against their androgyny. With its careful, small pleats at the shoulder, the circular neckline and rounded collar reminiscent of the 1950s blouses of Betty Draper. This impression was shattered like the hotel windows when earlier that day, a small German woman on the train had addressed them as though they were a young man when she asked Seasonal to help her lift her suitcase onto the luggage rack.

László kneels on the hardwood floor of the tastefully decorated room overlooking Oranienplatz.

I want to ask you to mark my body, he says, taking an eyeliner pencil from his pocket.

They both wonder if this subtle shift in who writes will change anything. Seasonal likes the idea.

The second time you marked your body for me, you marked the bottom of your foot. I found this placement quirky, and delightful. Please take off your shoes.

He obeys. They push him onto the king-size bed and grab his ankle as though he is a horse they are about to shoe.

They write in bold capital letters, in the center of the arch of his right foot: *YES.*

They two of them lie back and slowly remove their clothes. They lie in silence together on the overpriced bed.

Finally, László speaks. *I have a desire I would like to bring you.*

He looks up from their small breast, brings his face closer to theirs, and smiles through his eyes.

We have not made love, in the most traditional sense, and I would like to do that with you. I want to find a way to physically experience the gentleness. His voice is misty, he touches Seasonal's body as though it is blown glass.

They think it is not the right time, and make a lighthearted joke about the compelling monologue he gave them about how interesting it is not to fuck them when they were in Tilburg. He laughs.

It would be beautiful, he says, rubbing the head of his erection against their opening.

They have no doubt it would be. But that is a beauty they know, they have known many times in the past. It is a beauty they value very highly. But what he offers them is a rarer, more elusive thing—a thing they have not experienced, but which his submission makes them believe exists. They can't tell him what it is; Seasonal does not know its form yet. The possibility of discovering its form is why they are here. Their intuition tells them something is there, just out of reach, as it has repeatedly told them in relation to him. There is something *else,* beside, behind the forms of beauty and tenderness and hardness and freedom they have each known, with others, through their bodies before.

As it gets close to 3:00 a.m., he coaxes their need. They want him. They enjoy the wanting, but will not surrender to it. They are not interested in making love to someone else's partner. Just as they were not interested in being H's partner if he could not make love to them.

In the morning while he snores, Seasonal moves quietly around the bed to pick up their laptop from the bedside table. A large steel cock ring sits on top of it, the silvers of the devices matching perfectly, reflecting the dawn. Underneath the laptop sits the letter he wrote them. They open and read it while he sleeps. In his letter László writes with gratitude, and with a plaintive request for their patience as he attempts to find a way to repay them for all they have taught him.

What I feel now is what I felt when my headlamp switched off in the middle of a vast cave: that there is an immense wonderful world breathing around me in the darkness.

Two hours later, the two of them leave the hotel and transfer Seasonal's bags to the apartment. Over a breakfast of vegan muesli (them) and an apple pastry (him), László tries to put some pieces together.

So many elements of the exchange threaten my integrity, he says after his second cup of coffee. They are perched on high stools, avoiding the morning light by sitting at the back of the café.

It threatens key parts of myself: my sense of my dominance, my will, how I relate to others, my emotional responses, my identity as a male ... as a man. ... I worry I will go insane ... I left Hungary to preserve my integrity. I left everything behind because I could not live in that political situation without compromising my core integrity. My submission is also a threat. I worry that in writing me, you will be showing me parts of myself that I do not want to see.

Seasonal wants to ask László why he does not want to see these parts, but they don't. They do not want to push. When he talks about

Hungary, they hear the loss in his voice. They see it in his body, its shifting posture. His loss of Hungary is not for them to know. He lets them glimpse it sometimes, he points to it, he occasionally lets them see the joy and pleasure that comes with thinking of the coffeehouses of Budapest, his friends who have known him for twenty-five years, the Hungarian writers he carries within him and how they wrote the city, the country, the culture, and its tensions. In these moments they think they catch a glimpse of the iron will he used to turn himself into a cosmopolitan intellectual, cut off from the deep resources of the place that grew him and where his charisma and intelligence could have been a shared resource of the community that made him.

They know, also, that like them, László takes a deep, abiding pleasure in being outside.

They wonder how his core integrity will be affected when he discovers that in writing his submission, they have collected together his self-descriptions. They know he is right to fear those descriptions, to see the mirror he has made through talking with them.

After breakfast, they find their way to Museum Island. They stand in the sun by the river, a few blocks from the Schinkel Pavillon, where Seasonal saw an exhibition of work by Louise Bourgeois with Y and her daughter last summer. Twelve months ago, they stood here, holding on, hoping. They were in a fight for their life. Like Bourgeois's fabric sculptures, Seasonal's seams were holding, but barely.

As they stand together on the bridge in the bright Berlin sun, remembering Bourgeois's shapes, Seasonal casts aside their reservations and tells him he is welcome to make love to them, if he can enter them from within his submission.

You cannot enter me out of revenge, for the pain I give you, from your entitlement. I want you to enter me from within your submission.

They have a strong suspicion he won't be able to do it. But they keep this to themself. He solemnly agrees. Over the coming days, he will struggle. Several times he will approach their body—after they have given him pain, after they have penetrated more deeply into his own body than he thought possible—and he will lie above or behind them. But his sex will betray him, as he wrestles emotionally and intellectually to find a way to enter the body of the woman to whom he is so grateful for all he has learned. Seasonal will realize that these failures—after each of which he will say *I'm sorry*—are among the most important lessons they are teaching him.

But now, he stands before them. His hands hang loose by his sides, his gaze cannot settle. When he meets their eyes, he is pleading.

I feel like a piece of meat being sized up for dinner, he says nervously.

I know the male gaze, I use it. But to be on the receiving end of it is a discomforting experience.

As they leave the river and keep walking, Seasonal quietly accepts what they have come to Berlin to teach him. And what form the lesson will take.

Back at the apartment, afternoon sun streams in the window, turning the high-gloss concrete floor to silver. László wants to show them the object he has made to bring him pain. He asks tentatively, with casual politeness tinged with formality:

Did you happen to bring the ring I left at your place?

They hope he does not see them flinch at the thought of having to give it up.

Oh no. Sorry. You should have told me you needed it, they say, drawing a cloak around their greed for the object with what they hope passes as nonchalance.

Do you want me to send it to you here?

No. No hurry. I just don't want to forget about it, that's all, he responds, effortlessly matching their casual air.

He has just explained why giving someone jewelry is a *difficult thing.* He had said something about imposing. Seasonal has not really heard him over the noise coming in through the apartment window which bounces around the cavernous space because of the polished concrete floor. This ambient noise combines with the cacophony made by their greed and drowns out almost everything. They have not understood what the imposition is or would be. But they know that the answer is too obvious to ask him to explain, and they cannot speak straight away, silenced by the thought of losing the ring.

László returns from the bedroom with the object he has made. He places it on the coffee table in front of Seasonal and looks at their face, hopefully. The object he has repurposed is a nail. It has been cut in half, and the pieces of nail are set opposite each other in the circumference of a wide silver ring, implying that the ring has been pierced and the shaft removed.

Where did you find the nail? They handle it with awe.

In the street where my parents live, he says matter-of-factly.

László explains his theory of the ring's use: the ring fits his finger, and he will wear it and Seasonal will guide his hand and the tip of the nail. They look at him sharply and laugh.

Oh no. We both know this ring is going on my finger, they say gleefully, slipping it on.

His eyes bulge. He looks pleasantly nervous. They let the object do the work of arousing him and lead him silently to the bedroom.

Afterward, László gazes at the ceiling, his hand resting in the semen smeared on his stomach. *When you fuck me,* he says thoughtfully, as though what he is trying to say is written there but he cannot read it without his glasses, *I experience a dual perspective ... Lying beneath you, I feel as though I inhabit the position of all my previous lovers— the women who have lain beneath me. They return to me, as a kind of composite, and ... I have an experience from what I imagine is their point of view ...*

He rolls on his side to face them.

At the same time ... I recognize myself in your position. The way you fuck me is the way I fuck. I recognize ... what it is you are doing, how you are moving ... And so ... I see something of myself in you, even while I am seeing you as you.

Seasonal looks at him, conscious of him looking at them. They know what he is saying, because when they make love to him this way, they see his experience from a perspective of knowing and at the same time they sense the echoes of the movements of their own lovers in their own body. In the upper-body strength required to hold oneself above or to brace behind the body of the other, in the new angle at which their leg muscles must work to support their hips as they move deeper inside him. László kneels before them, or lies beneath them, in poses that are unique to him and uniquely compelling because they are given form in the lines only his body can make. And yet the positions, the pleasures, the vulnerability, the openness, the submission they see written there is not only familiar but somehow also partly theirs.

The next day, Seasonal sits in the large living room reading about O. They pause their reading and ask László about his opinion of the role of the valets in the chateau where O is initiated. The valets tend the submissives in their cells, chain them in the evening to the beds, and whip them when the masters cannot be bothered to administer punishment. The valets also have the discretion to use the bodies of the submissives when the masters are not present, and are instructed to ensure the submissives abide by the rule of silence, although they do this with varying degrees of strictness. Réage puts considerable care and skill into the characterization of the valets in the opening chapter. They are not mere functionaries, they are individuals. They approach their task, and use their discretion, uniquely. Seasonal wants to know what László thinks the role of the valet is—*Does a power exchange need a third?*

Joining them, naked, on the couch, László's answers:

The valets are the ones who do nothing about power. They do not think about it at all. The masters and the submissives are engaging it, its structure and function. The sad thing is that without the valets power would not exist in the first place.

They talk about Hannah Arendt, about the people who execute power without thinking about it. Seasonal thinks he is right, but they also wonder about the role of the valet as witness. If you read the first chapter of *The Story of O* as a crime novel, the valet bears witness to the crimes against O's freedom and bodily integrity that are committed. The valets are a necessary participating audience. They can confirm the nature of the experience the submissives are having but are also complicit in that experience, so cannot stand outside it and pass moral

(334)

judgement on the scene. Their presence is central to the humiliation of the submissives. The valet is the implicated subject—not the ultimate villain who enjoys ultimate power, nor the victim whose agency is entirely removed and subjugated. They do more than observe the scene; they play along.

In the shower the next morning, Seasonal wonders: *Why are the valets there? Are they paid? If so, do they receive holidays and sick leave? Is there a pension plan? Are the valets also submissives, held by the masters and enslaved through a parallel mechanism that is entirely invisible to O, and therefore to the reader? Are the valets recruited because they are subservient voyeurs, not smart enough to ascend to the role of dominant, but cruel and perverted enough to whip the submissives and ensure their adherence to rules they neither invented nor benefit from?*

After the shower the two of them agree to walk. Sitting high above the street, looking out onto the trees of Kreuzberg, the sparsely furnished apartment is a kind of nowhere place where they are both learning about the elasticity of the exchange—its various levels of intensity, its capaciousness, its flexibility. Now they are curious to be in public together, to see how it feels there. They rarely do this in the Netherlands, as their meetings are short and once they have walked the streets together at the beginning there is rarely time to be in the world in their respective roles.

László wants to show Seasonal *The Garden of Exile*, an artwork outside the Jewish Museum of Berlin. *Whenever I am in Berlin I come here*, László tells them as they walk the noisy, hot streets toward the garden.

The Garden of Exile is designed to produce disorientation. Tall concrete pillars in a tight grid tower above the visitor, limiting the view of the sky. The ground in the garden slopes at a twelve-degree angle. Walking within or around the small gridded space, it is not possible to get your bearings—there is no horizontal line available to anchor your vision.

Inside the garden, Seasonal feels instantly nauseous and disoriented. Standing deep within the grid, or at its edge and looking along the rows, does not alleviate the sense of claustrophobia and tiltedness.

After some time exploring the garden alone, they find each other at an intersection of two rows in the grid. Seasonal leans against a pillar, feeling gravity gently pulling their back onto the cool, hard surface.

Amazing, they say to him, grateful.

I brought you here because you are an exile now too, right?

Seasonal does not know how to answer him.

After finding a way out of the garden, walking toward a more conventional green space where they can sit beneath carefully trained trees also planted in a grid, Seasonal asks László about his previous visits here. He tells them that he first saw *The Garden of Exile* when he was still living in Hungary. When he was struggling to work out if he could stay there.

He visited again after he had moved to the Netherlands.

I almost vomited that time. The pain, the loss, was still so present.

This time he comes to *The Garden of Exile* to understand the disorientation of his submission.

Later, after more walking and talking in the hot streets of Berlin, they sit side by side on a bench on the street, eating pho in silence. László sips his beer quietly. They look at each other and smile. He sips his beer again and says, tentatively:

This is a little bit sad. But it is true. One of the things I learned this week is how to genuinely smile.

Seasonal returns his smile and looks out on the street, watching the children run in circles in the small park opposite the Vietnamese restaurant.

What am I in exile from? The Republic of Gender? Seasonal is thinking about her father, about rage, about Australia … they feel small and lost. They are grateful not to be sitting opposite him. They can ask him the question because they do not have to look at his face while they ask it.

His silence makes Seasonal afraid that he thinks their question is stupid. Shame begins to flood their body. Then he responds.

It is not the Republic of Gender. It is a People's Republic, László explains. *I come from a former People's Republic. It was the standard way that Communist dictatorships perverted the idea of the Republic in Soviet countries. It is anything but the people's. China is a People's Republic,*

North Korea is a People's Republic. Gender is also a People's Republic. It has nothing to do with the people.

They return to the apartment and lie in the heat together, exploring the possibility of the ring. As he opens his legs for them with sweet joy and Seasonal lowers their head alongside his and breathes their lust into his ear, he whispers, *I want to be your fuck toy.*

The next morning, László sits naked at his laptop in the living room. Seasonal lies in the bedroom, reading about O and listening to his rapid typing. Their clitoris swells and yells for him. The combination of reading his desires and the sound of his writing is inexplicably and surprisingly erotic. They do not know why the sound of him pounding the keys has this effect. It is 9:00 a.m.

To appease their lust, they walk into the room and interrupt him by putting the cuffs on his wrists. He is surprised, his body is a question. He is accustomed to having his work time respected. He smiles, and says:

Thank you.

They leave him to work some more and return to the bedroom. An hour passes, they read more about O, they look at the ceiling, they feel in the deep recesses of their desire, in their cunt and on their skin, that they will lead him here and without saying anything, lay him on his stomach and penetrate him with their double dildo. As their desire swells, they ponder their boundaries: *Can I?*

The short movement it takes to stand up and cross the threshold of the bedroom door provides the answer. All these months insisting that László bring them his desire have served a purpose. His desire for submission has been an acid. It has eroded the shell that encased their lust for the male body.

They collect him from the desk with a smile that he innocently returns and lead him to the bedroom. They push him onto his stomach. He lies face down with his legs spread on the bed, and they stand behind him, looking down at his prostrate body. They insert the female end of the dildo, it expands their desire but does not fill their need. They slip their legs into the harness and adjust the Velcro straps. They momentarily hope that László comes to associate the sound of Velcro with being violated. With a perfunctory gesture they smear some lubricant on the dildo. They pause and look down at his body. His face in the sheets. He is deathly still. They have not needed to restrain him. And they have not said a word.

Seasonal kneels between his legs and pushes into his body, laying their torso on his. They watch his face over his shoulder at close proximity. His eyes bulge in pain, he cries out as they push deeper into him. His face reddens. Their cunt floods around the dildo. They push harder and deeper, fascinated by the struggle that plays out across his face. Confusion and pain take over his features. The confusion is multifaceted. At the surface, he must acknowledge that he is being taken without consideration or care. Yet below this disorienting experience is the deeper confrontation they seek to occasion, and which is the true force of his subjection. As they continue to thrust into his body, he cannot reconcile his desire to protect himself from being penetrated with the bodily pleasure they are bringing him. The dissonance is written across his being: eyes screwed shut, face contorted in pain and anguish, his right hand moves to their buttocks to push them deeper inside him. His hips become more committed to meeting their movement.

They pull him up onto his knees and commandingly place their hands on his hip bones. They add more force to their thrust, allowing themself to enjoy the feeling of their power to bring him this pleasure. They run their right hand down the long, broad expanse of his back.

Then return their hand firmly to the curve where the shoulder meets the neck and leverage their hips against his body, increasing the force with which they move inside him. He moans loudly in the shape of a question. His breathing becomes labored, each exhale accompanied by a short sound, a kind of plea, that they have never heard from him before. His breath falls in time with the thrusting of their hips, and they know they have him in a new place.

Seasonal is determination. They are driven by their respect and compassion for him, and by their own unbearable passion to possess him. They thrust with more force and speed into his body, forcing his breath to change. He is no longer in control of his breathing or his body, he cries out in confusion and ecstasy.

They slow their movement within him, and withdraw quickly. A single sob escapes him. He lies beneath them, his body slack, his eyes closed. His devastation is palpable.

After some time, he speaks. *May I go now?* he says, almost inaudibly, into the sheets.

Yes.

With this they release him.

He stands up from the low bed and almost falls over. Seasonal lays on their back, their hands behind their head, curious about what they have just done, about what comes next. The coolness of their curiosity surprises them. They do not recognize this detachment.

Are you OK? they ask gently.

He shakes his head slowly. His voice is small.

No.

László stumbles to the bathroom, eyes dazed. Seasonal hears the shower running. The soap and shampoo bottle crash to the floor, the sound bouncing loudly in the small tiled space.

They await his return, coolly observing what is unfolding.

He leaves the bathroom and floats into the kitchen in a fog. They follow him and watch him drink a glass of water. His face is wrought by confusion and he is shaking.

What do you need? they ask softly.

He cannot respond. They take him in their arms in a solid embrace, and lead him gently back to the bed. He resumes the still pose he took earlier—on all fours, buttocks in the air, face in the mattress.

There is more than one sob now.

When I sought my annihilation, I had no idea what it was I was seeking, he says, his wet face in the blue sheets.

László arrived at the destination that had been calling him, tantalizing him. The place he thought might exist, if he could find the guide and the path, and if he could walk the path once it was shown to him. The place he had been curious about for who knows how long. The idea of this place had taken him to play parties where he had been disappointed and turned-off by the aesthetics. It had led him to offering his body to people he did not trust, to being tied and beaten and electrocuted by them and wondering why he was unsated. The hunch he had about this place led him to the internet to say *Hello, World?* with a picture of Michel Foucault and inaccurate self-descriptions to see if his guide would appear.

When Seasonal arrived as his guide, he described the place he was hoping to find. They agreed to lead him there, knowing full well that the location he envisioned and longed for was not where he was going.

As he cries into the sheets next to their naked body, entirely bereft of any sense of his identity, his anchor taken away by shock and ecstasy, they know that he is crying from the realization that the place is not a place at all.

Thank you, he says, dazed.

They place their hands lightly on the tops of his arms and seek his eyes.

Are you OK? they ask again.

Yes. Can I ask you to hold me?

Within minutes he is asleep in their arms.

When he wakes up, they lay their naked bodies together. He thanks them again. His smile is serene and wide. He looks softly into their eyes and tells them he knows they approached, or breached, a number of their boundaries in what they just did.

Can you name them for me? Seasonal's voice is small. They need to hear him speak the words that are ringing in their ears.

In his calm, deep timbre he says plainly:

Rape, sexual assault, disregard for the other, disinterest in consent. He pauses. Then a smile crosses his face, his voice gains a spring as he says:

Essentially: male sexuality.

Seasonal is silent. They cannot look at him. They feel that trying to know men is like trying to see what is in their peripheral vision. Knowledge of men is constantly evading their attempts to master it. Is this why they have tried to occupy the role themself?

They are dumb. Their mouth feels as though it is full of thin grey ash.

László asks Seasonal to make love to him. He is reaching for the dildo with a smile. They are surprised and want to give him what he asks for. He smiles through his eyes as they move slowly within him. Afterward, he happily announces that the two of them should find something to eat. They dress efficiently and begin searching the neighborhood for food.

Two blocks east of the apartment they arrive at a café with tables on the street corner. On butcher's paper in the window is a sign handwritten in big red letters: *No Place for Toxic Masculinity.*

After what you did this morning, László quips, *I don't think you can eat here.*

Seasonal's laugh rings out, tinged with incomprehension and shamelessness. The two of them take a seat at a table that has just become free on the shady side of the building.

That evening, sitting in Tian Fu in some distant part of Berlin, the Sichuan beef strips languish, uneaten, in front of László. The two of them assess the morning together.

I just thought a sentence I never thought I would think in my life... Seasonal says, and sees their smile reflected on his face.

Tell me, he says.

I can't say it here. They nervously cast a glance at the couple with two children eating at the adjacent table.

Say it, he says with honey in his voice to coax them.

I just thought: If I could rape you every day this week, I would be happy.

What? he says, leaning in.

If I could rape you every day this week, I would be happy, they repeat with surprising ease.

He smiles with his whole body. They look with wonder into their small cup of jasmine tea in its pristine white porcelain.

The conversation circles around Seasonal's pleasure. László begins a long monologue unwinding the possibility that Seasonal is much better at dominance, and has fewer resistances about violence, than they think. Seasonal cannot really follow him, until he says these words:

... your identity as a rapist ...

The food turns in Seasonal's stomach. They put their face in their hands. The floor drops out from under them and they are adrift. Shame. Horror. They are lost.

… your identity as a rapist …

A few minutes later, they are standing on the street, having fled the restaurant after paying the bill. László stands before them.

They speak the truth quickly followed by a lie.

You were coming at me pretty hard in there. I can take it …

They try to find their way back to the truth, because they know it is the only way to find the trust they need to have in him now.

… but you really don't need to come after me like that.

They look around the street, avoiding his eyes.

He apologizes. In their hand, Seasonal holds their phone, its screen displaying Google Maps. The directions showing the dotted line they need to walk to the subway station emit a soft and reassuring glow. They stare at the screen. The map bears no useful information, but in this moment they do not trust László to tell them where they are. They focus on the blue dot on the map and try to locate themself.

May I hug you? he asks cautiously.

They consent. As his arms close around them, Seasonal tries to let the meeting of their bodies emplace them. They try to feel his weight. It does nothing. They breathe in the smell of his T-shirt. It does nothing.

They break the embrace and stare out across the street at the nondescript Berlin neighborhood, made up of low-rise buildings rendered in beige and cream. There is no graffiti in this part of the city. All they see are walls, and windows through which no light passes. They vaguely sense people passing by on the sidewalk. They have a dim awareness that László is looking at their face. Looking at the pavement, seeking desperately any information that will give them a sense of place, Seasonal's thumb instinctively wakes up their phone. Their gaze returns to the screen and the blue dots that promise guidance, locatedness. They look at it, helpless. László gently takes the phone from their hand and slips it in the pocket of his linen pants. He puts his hand in its place. It is a foreign object, out of focus.

You have my full trust and consent, he says slowly and earnestly.

They try to hear him.

I want to say it again. Into your eyes.

The instruction reaches Seasonal's ears with soft insistence.

Raising their head takes all their remaining energy. The vertebrae in their neck complain bitterly at being issued the task of lifting the useless weight of their head. They face him, and he repeats firmly:

You have my full trust and consent.

Thank you, they say meekly, holding his eyes.

Nothing you have done with me has anything to do with abuse, he says with certainty.

I have no idea how it is that, with your history, you are so strong, and so powerful. I have no experience of what you have told me about, I cannot imagine it. I am in awe of what you have made of yourself from it. And to use the power you have the way you do … he trails off, unable to find the termination of this sentence.

Seasonal knows that the root of their power begins before any conscious memory. It is their very condition. They wish that him saying this could reconnect them to their sense of who they are. But what they have done has stripped away the veneer. All the reading, fantasies of mastery through writing and talking with László were undoing one story and writing another. But the suspension of disbelief they had built through the power exchange was punctured by his casual labeling: *your identity as a rapist.* They had crossed a threshold and now they were totally lost.

Seasonal looks at László's caring, open face and pretends to feel a little better. They pretend in order to weaken the fear of being lost, they pretend out of gratitude for his support and care, they pretend because they cannot stand on this street forever, they pretend because something has to happen to get them moving toward the safety of the apartment, where they can sink into the oblivion of their shame and horror in peace and quiet. They long for the apartment in order not to long for death.

On the return journey on the subway, László sits an arm's length from them on the long bench seat in the half-empty carriage and rests a hand on their shoulder. They feel a slow return. He tells them as the train crosses the city that they have liberated him through their dominance, through what they did this morning. By the time they are walking toward the apartment, they realize what they need to ask him.

I have a question, which might also be a request. Normally it is I who lead, that is the dom's job.

They swallow the sharp bile that rises in their throat.

But I am wondering: Can the submissive lead the dom toward liberation?

His answer is affirmative:

You have taught me so much today. I will never look at sex the same way again. You have taught me compassion.

Seasonal barely hears him. They feel themself emptying again. Their body is nothing, their mind blank, they are nowhere. They feebly walk alongside him, drowning. They put one foot in front of the other in the service of their only need—to be off the street, to be somewhere private, to be somewhere where they will have the silence they need to reorient themself.

They must accept László as their guide, gently taking them to privacy. They follow him numbly, looking at the pavement, feeling only the familiar and comforting rhythm of their legs in motion and their feet hitting the hard surface.

Without warning, László abruptly stops.

I just have to go in here quickly, he says lightly, standing in the brightly lit doorway of a store.

They nod distractedly and keep walking. As they walk past the closed shopfronts and graffitied doors of apartment buildings, their eyes well.

No, Seasonal says aloud. With a shaking hand they reach for the cigarettes in their bag to fortify themself against the tears. *No*, they think again. *The dom cannot cry.*

The next morning, while László snores musically beside them, Seasonal checks Facebook. A great novelist, Toni Morrison, has died. Seasonal's feed is awash with dedications to her body of work. One quote recurs again and again as they scroll:

… if you are free, you need to free somebody else.

Later that morning, László sits at the dining table in the rented apartment watching Seasonal pack the chain, the cuffs, the small padlocks, and the rope into the duffle bag. He is wearing a linen T-shirt of khaki that perfectly mediates between his dark skin and green eyes. He is watching them, hoping they will take the copy of Beauvoir's essay out of their bag and leave it for him.

That is a big ask, they say as they zip their small toiletries bag.

You have no idea how difficult it is for me to leave behind a book I am still reading, that I feel still has so much to offer me.

They had made little progress with Beauvoir since the train, spending most of their time reading *O*.

But of course he knows. And he is happy with his victory when they put the book on the dining table.

I keep saying thank you. It feels ridiculous, but I am also constantly scared that I am not saying it enough, he says, smiling at the incongruity as they stand together.

This is submission, they explain.

The dom is never satisfied, and the sub never satisfies their need to show gratitude. It is perpetual and unavoidable.

Thank you for explaining that to me.

Do you remember what I told you about repetition and dominance, right at the beginning?

Yes, he smiles.

Say it all you want.

Seasonal puts on their shoes.

Do you mind if I don't walk to the station?

Sure. I get the impression you don't like train stations much, Seasonal says as they tie their shoelaces, remembering his first visit to Utrecht and his request to meet somewhere *less stressful and transitory.*

No, I don't like them. And I do not like sad goodbyes. The light in his eyes dims.

Dear Seasonal, the
marks you left on
my body are turning
dark and rough.
The sudden silence
is painful. Your
scent is fading.

Nothing will be
the same again.

Thank you.

Epilogue: Keep Looking

A month later Seasonal will fly to Berlin, hire a car, and drive with László to a hunter's cabin on the edge of a forest in the east of Germany. They will have a long weekend in a space where László does not need to be gagged, replacing the anonymity of the city with the anonymity of the German countryside and the freedom of no neighbors. They will arrive with a willful determination to hear him scream, to take him back to Hungarian—as they had when they hung him from the tethers in their apartment.

They have come back to Germany because they want to make him bleed. They have a plan for this too. But on the second day, after they have strung him from the solid pine beam that spans the bedroom and laid down the marks that they intend to reopen the next day, László will be struck by a stomach bug and will be barely conscious for twenty-four hours. He will lie in the sun in the yard and tentatively take a walk with them in the afternoon. They will have fucked him out of annoyance that morning, which he liked but which also made him think about all the times his partner had allowed him to fuck her because it was easier to be fucked than not.

Before they check out of the cabin and drive into the mountains for lunch on their return to Berlin Tegel Airport, he will give them a long monologue in response to their concern about the ethics of using his body as vehicle for their frustration.

This is what it is to have a dick, he will say with his plain-speaking charisma.

Everything in the world tells you to have a dick means you have to put it somewhere. That every scene of sexuality is about your dick. He goes on to tell them how hard it is for men—thinking men, who realize that this is no longer an acceptable way to be—to find something else to do with their dicks. Seasonal will find his earnest and extended elucidation of this problem, and his seeming expectation of their sympathy for the plight of dick owners, ludicrous. They will tell him so.

They will fly back to the Netherlands having failed to make him bleed. Their plans foiled by his weak constitution.

A few weeks after their failed visit, László will travel to Hungary to see his parents. Seasonal will travel to Copenhagen to speak at a conference about literature. He will message them from the airport as he waits for the plane that will bring him back to the Netherlands.

Coming back here
and talking to friends
and family is like
going back to the
place and people where
violence was the norm.
I was subject to
violence, and I hurt
others. I left to
escape, but that did
not stop the violence
itself taking place
here.

So I'm now amongst
people who are victims
and perpetrators, often
at the same time,
and I see how that
violence slowly deforms
their faces, visits,
thoughts, emotions.

These are people I
loved, and people
I never met.

Being witness to
this tragedy kills
me. My helplessness
kills me.

All I could tell
people was that
they should run, as
fast as they could.

                                        Run to where?

Away from the place,
the contexts, which
turn them into
monsters.

                                        how does it feel
                                        to be leaving?

Betrayal and immense
liberation.

A few weeks later, Seasonal will finally slap László's face in public, fulfilling a shared desire. It will happen in a quiet residential street in Amsterdam, where the two of them are walking, discussing plans for how Seasonal might prostitute László.

I am going to slap your face now, they will say calmly.

I understand why it is necessary, he will respond, resigned.

They will pause, facing each other in the narrow street, running alongside the final yards of the Prinsengracht before it disappears into the IJ river. Thin two-story row houses, painted in black, blue, and ochre, lean on each other facing the canal. They have the posture of the inebriated British lads who walk in groups in the heart of the city at all times of the day and night. Look at them for long enough and you become convinced they will collapse. Each house is on its own particularly strange angle, reflecting the specific way its foundations are sinking into the watery terrain. When Seasonal strikes him, each house has its face in the early afternoon sun, some with their doors and shutters open to the light. The sharp sound of the slap will echo off the buildings and ricochet from the canal, and its complex timbre will be an unexpected delight to Seasonal. The intense high frequencies disappear quickly, but a darker tone will ring out in the street for a millisecond longer. The size and dimensions of the street will be written in sonar.

László's shock will be undeniable and immediate. He will work his jaw once or twice in a reflex action to check for damage. The skin on the palm of Seasonal's hand will tingle pleasantly with aftershocks. The entire inner side of Seasonal's hand will dance. They will smile broadly. A red mark will form on the right-hand side of László's face as the blood rushes to the large surface area which is the contact zone between his submission and their dominance.

Immediately after he receives the blow, they will resume walking up the deserted residential street in silence. The pale early-autumn light will glint softly on the canal. Each of them will occupy their side of the exchange: Seasonal will not be able to hide their pride at having overcome the safety catch on their annoyance and frustration; László will be far away, trying to reconstruct himself after this brush with the brute force of their power. His walking will be in a steady rhythm with theirs. He will keep pace.

They will periodically look at this face that bears their mark as they walk toward the river and glow in satisfaction, marveling.

I was not prepared for the force, he will admit later.

They were. It is the force they have been holding back from him from the beginning.

Sitting in front of a fire in a café on the IJ, after they have both recovered from the slap, their talk will return to when and how Seasonal will prostitute him, and whether or not their presence in the scene of his sexual service is necessary. László will say with breathtaking openness and sincerity:

The thing that appeals to me most about you whoring me is that you will fuck me afterward to take me back.

For the first time, Seasonal's heart will swell for him. They will see his desire to be more than tolerated and given permission to take his desire elsewhere. He will talk about wanting more than being forgiven. He will talk about shame, about sin, about forgiveness, about tolerance, and about the restrictive, thin nature of these positions. He will tell them that being their whore will give him the opportunity for some other relationship with his desire.

They will respond by agreeing that the whore (he) and the pimp (they) operate in these waters. *But these figures also—as sex worker advocates tell us—enact disruptive pleasures,* they tell him. They will not whore him out of sadism. They will whore him because he longs to be a whore, and they know he needs their dominance to authorize that desire. They will whore him because being a whore will bring him pleasure. They will whore him because finding an ethical way to experience true ownership of him will bring them to the realization of a desire they thought impossible and about which they have felt deep shame and trepidation. They will not say to him, in the late afternoon on the low-slung peach couch in front of the fire in the café, *I don't tolerate the whore in you, I admire and love him.*

The following morning, it will be 10:00 a.m. It will be a Monday. László will arrive at Seasonal's apartment wanting to be fucked, because he is *alone with my son until Wednesday* and he has begged to see them.

But when they lie together on Seasonal's too-big bed, László will pull their body toward him and slip his erection into their slick cunt. Seasonal will gasp from the fullness, and look to his face. The bright eyes they know will be replaced with wet discs that absorb rather than reflect the light. His gaze will be directed at them, but these are not looking eyes. They will be eyes that have learned to unsee because to see is to feel and to feel is to know and to know demands action.

As he fucks them, Seasonal will realize that László has chosen to betray himself—his desire, his need, his questions, his joy—rather than confront what he has chosen. He will fuck Seasonal from his self-betrayal, from the way he has learned to fuck outside his home to keep his home safe.

He will expertly angle his body to push his dick deeper into them, monitoring with a detached but precise attention how his movement enhances their pleasure. Seasonal will hear the rust-and-silver ring hit the oak headboard as he pulls on it to increase his force. Like a well-trained gymnast, working from muscle memory rather than expression, he will be silent, joyless, determined. A simulacra of passion.

Seasonal will look into the dead eyes of self-betrayal—the eyes of their mother, the eyes H hid behind while he refused to answer their questions about his disappeared desire—and they will wonder where the man they know has gone: the man on the beam, the man in their hands, the one who shone when he asked to be fucked. Their heart will plummet with the realization that László has already made himself a fuck toy, has already sought and found the safety of being owned by another's desire, because he cannot bear the possibility of owning himself.

They will watch him as he works at fucking them, taking his pleasure while pretending to be interested in theirs. He will not be able to get deep enough. He will not have the power or the attention they need. Unlike when he uses his hands, when he uses his small reserves of humility, they will not feel his power or his intention. Looking at his face as he continues the robotic gestures of this kind of sex that he is familiar with, Seasonal will briefly face who they chose not to become when they could not accept H's invitation for an open relationship. As he climaxes, László will pull out of their body, abruptly shortening their pleasure with his sudden withdrawal. He will cover their stomach with semen. They will wonder why he did not use a condom and dimly remember the decades of boring conversations they've had with men about safe sex and whose responsibility it is.

Afterward, they will lie together on their backs, quietly watching the sun move across the sky. And then he will abruptly say, *I have to go*.

Seasonal will be annoyed and surprised. Here is the story they have been trying to avoid from the beginning: a married man rushing out of their apartment to collect his son from school. After he has left, Seasonal will look at themself in the mirror and not like what they see.

Seasonal will try desperately to redirect the story. To shift the narrative away from reality, back to fantasy. To disentangle themself from the mess that is not theirs. They will want to describe the two cats in the dream, the *I* that is *playing with each other*. They will spend the evening working on a soliloquy which they send via WhatsApp around 12:00 a.m.

> *i know that making
> love to me the
> way you did
> yesterday was simply
> a means of you
> being present in
> your desire for
> me and your interest
> in our mutual
> pleasure. but in
> making love to me
> that way, you
> returned me to the
> countless moments in
> my sexual life where
> i embraced conventional
> pleasures—the
> low-hanging fruit
> of my eroticism.*

in making love
to me that way
you also reminded
me of my own
complicity and self-
betrayal; the regularity
with which i
banish my desire
and perversion from
the erotic scene.

the desire i bring
to my exchange with
you, ultimately,
is that i do not
want to betray
the pervert in me
any longer.

but i also have
to say that i
could not make
love to you in the
scene that unfolded
yesterday because i
have agreed not to
love you. not to
want you, not to
need whatever power
being loved by you

might provide, because
i want to be
able to roam free
in my perversion
with you. i also
agreed not to love
you out of respect
for your commitment
to your family. i
could not enjoy
making love to
you out of my
desire to be loved,
out of my desire
to be lost in
the pleasure of being
possessed by you,
because the exchange
and the terms we
agreed on require that
(of me and the kind
of person i am,
at least).

it is your desire
to be possessed
that drives the
passion in our
exchange, not
mine.

i could not
make love to
you from within
that desire—in
all its brilliance,
familiarity, capacity
to anchor and enable
me—because it
is known, and
because it is
excluded from the
exchange as i
understand it. and
because i am
bringing to you my
desire for uncharted
territories and freedom.

A silence will open between them that Seasonal finds a huge relief. They will understand they have failed. They will return to the rhythm of their life. The blister they became when H left has burst. They are raw, new skin. Too tender for the world. Their experiment in extreme intention gave them the protection they needed to heal. They are ready to face the possibility of being shattered by the other, rather than only being the force that shatters. They can face the possibility of reciprocity, they want to find again the horror and joy of the universe through someone's body, rather than stage it through the theatre of domination. They sit in the weakened sun that heralds the beginning of the season the Dutch call *herst*, Americans call *fall*, and Australians call *autumn*. They wonder why there are so many names for this moment of transition. In Australia very little falls, but in the streets and parks of Utrecht, the leaves are beginning the invisible process of loosening their hold on the trees. Seasonal looks at the tall plane trees that stand outside the Utrecht city archives, and accepts two truths. One old, one new. Both truths are born of failure, and are therefore precious. The old truth was learned through their childhood, when they thought their love could free their mother from the misery of her marriage, of their family. Seasonal accepts again, today, that bearing attentive witness to another's pain and wanting more for them than the pain they mistake for love can have no effect. The second truth is what László has made of them. They must face their fate and be the person he has helped them become.

While Seasonal looks at trees, László's erection is straining against his jeans. He is not wearing underwear, and the proximity of the metal zipper to this most tender part of him makes him feel virtuous, almost holy. One by one he takes his son's T-shirts from the drying rack and folds them neatly. As he folds each one, László recalls a moment from the past two weeks in which his son had worn the shirt he now holds in his hands. This yellow one, almost too small for him now, he wore last Saturday to a friend's house. He had come home beaming, full of details of action in Fortnite. László had listened and smiled as the description tumbled from the boy's mouth, almost too fast for him to enunciate the words, frantically seeking the ear of the father. This blue-and-white-striped one, warm from the sun, the boy had thrown across the room in light frustration as he prepared for bed on Tuesday, complaining bitterly about the tests he must do the next day at school. László had calmly picked it up, reassuring his son that tomorrow was something he could face. After the boy felt secure and went to sleep, László had spent a few hours working on his book about the internet, climbed into bed beside his partner, and slept a blissful sleep.

László has traded his shame for a secret. It is a real secret because it is shared with only one person. László feels light, relieved, because someone knows the man he is when he asks for more pain, the man he is when he asks sweetly for his body to be filled, the man he is in his aching, vulnerable need to be restrained and overwhelmed, the man he is when he fails to fuck a woman the way a man should want to, the man he is when he surrenders his struggle for freedom. This shared secret with Seasonal deepens his sense of purpose and makes each part of his life bright with his knowledge of the truth.

As he picks up a red T-shirt, his memory shifts from his son to the first time Seasonal made love to him. László has recalled this moment many times since it first happened, almost a year ago. It is the memory of meeting himself, learning who he is. Today his mind writes the memory in English, to give him the added excitement of imagining that Seasonal is listening to his thoughts. He wants to transmit to Seasonal what he cannot say. He knows that after thinking these thoughts, he will go to the bathroom and furiously masturbate, recalling the bliss of giving himself to Seasonal. He will try to give himself that bliss and peace with his own hand, and he will fail.

ACKNOWLEDGEMENTS

When I realized that I was writing a novel, I was spurred on by the hope that maybe I could become Lauren Berlant's second-favorite sex writer. Instead, I have learned to accept the space they left behind, and to struggle on with the questions their writing and conversation ignited in me.

I started writing in 1995 to survive the loss of Angie Lamb, and all my books are in some way testament to what she gave me during her short life.

Bodó Balázs, Michelle Dicinoski, Ali Alizadeh, Catherine Strong, Oscar Schwartz, Marcus Kuijper, Kathrin Thiele, and Kiene Brillenburg Wurth read early versions of the manuscript and were precious interlocutors. Thanks to Anthony Pateras for solidarity and belief, Carlie Lazar for life-sustaining laughter, and Paul Byron for walks and questions.

I am indebted to Chris Kraus for calling my bluff and asking to see the manuscript long before it was ready, and for subsequent provocations and illuminating editing. Thank you to Robert Dewhurst for smoothing wrinkles I mistakenly thought were permanent, and to Lauren Mackler for the beautiful design using a photograph by Samantha Arnull.

And thank you, Samantha Arnull and Quinn Eades, for the love.

ABOUT THE AUTHOR

For over twenty years, Anna Poletti has researched how media shapes the meaning we attach to lived experience. Her recent books include *Stories of the Self: Life Writing after the Book* (2020) and the Eisner Award–nominated collection *Graphic Medicine* (coedited with Erin La Cour, 2022).